T0146991

PULL

ME

IN

# PULL ME IN

## KYLA OLIVER

iUniverse

# PULL ME IN

*iUniverse books may be ordered through
booksellers or by contacting:*

*iUniverse
1663 Liberty Drive
Bloomington, IN 47403
www.iuniverse.com
1-800-Authors (1-800-288-4677)*

*Because of the dynamic nature of the Internet, any web
addresses or links contained in this book may have changed
since publication and may no longer be valid. The views
expressed in this work are solely those of the author and do
not necessarily reflect the views of the publisher, and the
publisher hereby disclaims any responsibility for them.*

*Any people depicted in stock imagery provided
by Getty Images are models, and such images are
being used for illustrative purposes only.
Certain stock imagery © Getty Images.*

*ISBN: 978-1-5320-7556-8 (sc)
ISBN: 978-1-5320-7557-5 (e)*

*Print information available on the last page.*

*iUniverse rev. date: 05/21/2019*

*Insomniac*

*Sleepless nights go by unnoticed...*
*Since the tables have turned*
*I've all of a sudden developed this*
*feeling of reasonable doubt.*
*Lay my head down on my bed*
*Close my eyes to realize*
*That I can't sleep,*
*The thought of you not here with me is making me weak.*
*An insomniac is just a maniac!*
*Sitting up in my bed,*
*I see the fiery hells of red!*
*Insomniac! Insomniac!*
*I cannot sleep until you are here,*
*Holding me, healing me*
*Keeping my head clear.*
*To help me forget the perfection that I lack,*
*To help me to forget, I am an insomniac.*

Spring 1985

Every passing day is a blessing for me. All that I've been through and everything that I've done in my life, this far, has almost become too much to bare. I get so upset with myself for not believing I could overcome any obstacle. I lock myself away and hide me from the rest of the world. Weeks go by when I'm barricaded inside of my own home, day in and day out. Crying myself to sleep night and night again. There's something missing. A simple knock at the door sounds more and more familiar each time. I wish I had someone who could truly understand how I feel. So much so, feelings of overwhelming dread crowd my soul. I try to remember to be thankful as I drag through every day feeling jailed, caged, and destined to be alone with myself only. *Sigh* I don't want to live like this anymore. Getting to sleep is difficult for me and staying asleep has become even harder. My heart is filled with anxiety I feel like my head is going to explode. The excitement of getting to school and away from home builds me up. Sigh I tossed and turned in my sheets as I grew more and more anxious. It's one o'clock in the morning, I only have a few hours until six o'clock to race mom out of the house. If she stops me just short of twisting the door knob I'm never going to school again.

I'm Stacy Viera. I was born and raised in the Rockies right in the heart of Denver. I love my city! I mean, this is where all my friends and family are. The family that I know about at least. Nevertheless, this place is where my heart belongs. Just me and my momma, Terry, in my daddy's house, really. His name is, Charles. I guess we would go and visit him a while back when I was a kid, but I don't remember going. No one ever told me exactly what he did or why we can't go see him anymore. Whenever I ask my momma all she says is I'm too young to understand; maybe I am. Lately, no one talks about him at all.

I was twelve years old when Grandma Sarah, my moms' mom, told me Dad was in "college." Once I stopped believing that, I stopped asking. Although, she does reassure me he was a good man and nothing less. I still wonder about him. I wonder what he sounds like? How Dad walks the walk? It makes me wonder if he's even alive. Maybe Mom and Grandma think I'm not strong enough to handle that. If only my Dad could see me now. I'm sure that he wouldn't be very proud of me. Though, all I want is to hear him tell me how much he loves me and to be a good girl. I wish he was here with us every single day. Some days

I wish he would just write to me or call. If he was here I probably wouldn't be in the situation I'm in.

Footsteps began to creep up toward my bedroom. Mom's about to curse me out about something. Ugh I cleaned both bathrooms, the kitchen and the living room. Everything except for my room. I squeezed my eyes shut and threw the covers over my head as the door slowly opened. Who I believed to be my mother sat comfortably behind my knees, the pressure of their body was crushing as they softly pulled the sheets from my face.

"Wake up, baby," the deep, chilling tone spoke quietly.

My eyes grew wide. There was Sammy, smiling at me through the darkness. Without his pale white shirt or shinning golden teeth I wouldn't have seen him. I was confused and a little afraid. Happy, though very curious as to how the hell he got into my house. Let alone all the way up into my bedroom without waking up my mother across the hall. She would flip.

I angrily whispered, "Sammy, what are you doing? How'd you get in here?"

"Mom," he said with confidence, "Come on, get dressed we're waiting for you outside."

"Who?" I questioned before pausing to think, "Wait, I have to go to school in the morning."

"I'll bring you right back," Sammy assured me as he rose to his feet, "Just come on."

Like a snake he slithered out the door. He's lying, my mother would never let him in at this time of night. Still, I scurried out of my pajamas and into my clothes. Quietly slipping out of my room and across the hall to check on my mother. I slowly twisted her knob and poked my head in. She was sound asleep. Weird, maybe she was so incoherent she just opened the door for him came back and went to sleep. Like she was sleep walking or something. I rushed outside and forgot all about Mom once I seen Janessa in Sammy's Chevrolet.

"Hey! Hurry up, hurry up get in!" Janessa shouted quietly.

Janessa's arms flailing with the door wide open. Wow, I recognized her new style before her. She looks like a grown woman with her new weave standing up on her head. I dashed down the driveway and into the backseat.

"Ness!" I said aloud, "Hey, Terrell."

"What's up, Stace," Terrell responded, "Look like you getting thick little mama."

Janessa rolled her eyes and curled up her nose in disgust behind Terrell's head. I laughed to myself as I playfully slapped her thigh.

"I missed you, friend where have you been?"

"I missed you, too," I responded, my head low, "Don't ask."

"Call me next time you get locked up and I'll come bust you out," Janessa joked.

We laughed aloud as Sammy and Terrell chattered over the sound of us. I have missed this crazy girl. I haven't seen her since before spring break started.

"Waffles?" Sammy interrupted, slightly peering back at us "Yeah?"

We quickly straightened up, "Yeah, baby, that sounds good."

"I guess," Janessa responded, "I thought that we were going to do something better than that."

Terrell swiftly looked back to Janessa, "What's that?"

She put on the fakest smile I had ever seen and closed in on Terrell as if she was going for a kiss, "Let's smoke."

Terrell went for Janessa's lips just before she pulled back and plopped down beside me, "not now, but now, baby."

Janessa and I giggled as they each locked eyes. Sammy chuckled to himself before starting up the engine he ripped away from the curb, roaring down my street. *Ugh* I hate the sound of his car it's way too noisy. Sammy turned up the music so loud I couldn't even hear my own thoughts, only the vibrations of his base in my entire body. Terrell passed a thick, flaming joint over the seat back to Janessa. I still couldn't believe she had the power to wrap this man up. Although, it has been a little over a year now since we all first met.

"You ready for school tomorrow?" she leaned in to ask me.

"Yeah, I can't wait it's been a long week stuck at home," I responded.

"I can't wait to see, Dominic," she giggled, "He fought that other big, big boy before we started spring break."

"I know I was sitting right there," I told her.

"You don't see him after school?" Janessa nosily questioned.

"No."

"Why not?" she asked confused, "Is that because of your Momma, too?"

"Shut up," I giggled, "Talking about my Momma."

"She better let you come to school tomorrow or you're going to get held back," Janessa confessed, gazing at her long fingernails.

Without another word I glared out of my window; the smoke crowding my vision.

Sammy eased into a packed parking lot. There were so many Chevy's anything else pulling in would be shamed.

"The fight must be over," Terrell spoke.

I hate being next to the tracks down Peoria it's too dark and there are always some sketchy people hanging around the liquor store. Once inside, we were barely able to find a table as we squeezed down the rows pushing past loud mouths and basket weaves. The gangsters came out tonight and they came out deep. Though, they soon became obsolete once the waitress took our orders and brought the waffles.

"It's only like two o'clock, let's go back to my cousin's party," Janessa randomly pressed Terrell.

"Go back?" I questioned, looking to Sammy for answers.

Sammy put his face in the plate and continued eating as if he didn't hear me. Now, I was starting to get upset. They were all three in the car dressed and acting funky like they been up riding around all night before coming to get me.

"How long have you been with them tonight?" I asked Janessa.

"Girl, you can't go nowhere or do nothing, so I asked them to take me to my cousins party," Janessa spat.

"She was with me, Stacy and we're really not doing nothing so we can go back," Terrell agreed with Janessa.

"No, take me home," I demanded, putting on my coat, "Now, Sammy!"

"Damn, Stacy, chill out," Sammy finally spoke to me.

"Well, drop her off so we can go," Janessa demanded.

At this point I was blown away I couldn't believe my ears. I looked to Janessa with hurt in my eyes. As bad as I wanted to sit up there and start crying I wasn't going to do that. It was way too packed.

"Seriously, J," I questioned, confused, "Yup, drop me off now!"

Anguish filled my heart, I got up from the table and made my way out the door to Sammy's car. Janessa followed close behind, attempting to clean up what she said to me. Honestly, I think she was just trying to show out because all these fly guys are here. She looks like a new person, and now Janessa's acting like it. Terrell and Sammy stayed behind inside to wait on the check.

"Stace, listen to me please," she begged.

I shouted, "No! What happened the last time we all went to a party?" tears bursting from my face, "Seriously, J, you're my best friend you're supposed to have my back."

"I do that's why I was going to say just come and we'll all stay together this time," she responded clinging onto me.

It was like my friend was changing in front of my face. I was literally speechless. Sammy and Terrell started out the door towards the two of us waiting by the vehicle. I snatched my arm from Janessa's grasp, walked around to Sammy's side and got in the car.

"Janessa, leave her alone," Sammy demanded.

My anger was masked by the music, the entire way home I sat by Janessa in silence. My arms folded over my chest and all my attention on the stars. Janessa's jingling wrists annoyed me. Every now and then she would try to speak to me, but I have no more words. Sammy pulled up to my house slowly, then quickly turned to me just before I could get out. In an instant, he reached back over the sat and swatted Janessa's face. We gasped as Janessa's head hit the window. She placed a hand over her mouth and dropped her head in her lap. Terrell sat in silence, facing forward picking food out of his teeth.

"You need to learn when to shut your mouth," he scolded, his finger pointed boldly in her face, "I love you, Stacy, do you want me to stay?"

My jaw was on the floor. Without responding, I snatched the door handle and leaped out of the car. What the hell? Sammy just hit my friend with no hesitation.

"I'll see you at school tomorrow, best fri-."

Before Janessa could even finish her sentence. I slammed the door in her face and blocked them both out completely. Sammy started out of the car after me as I dashed to the front door. Frantic, I jiggled with the lock trying to get into my house. I glanced back at Sammy just a few feet away before leaping over the threshold and slamming the door tightly shut behind me.

# School Morning

"Stacy! Stacy!"

Its seven o'clock in the morning and my moms' voice is right on schedule screaming my name from down the hall. I couldn't help but attempt to ignore her as I stared hopelessly at the clock on my dresser. I sluggishly dragged myself out of my warm bed, huffing and groaning at the aches in my back and legs. After a minor stretch, I reluctantly picked up my school shirt from a pile of clothes on the floor. Nausea set in as I stood up right. Just like yesterday and the day before that. I think I need to eat something. Damn, I should have finished my waffles last night. As I paced my filthy bedroom floor for the rest of my uniform Mom swiftly opened my door and allowed herself in.

"Stacy!" she blared at me, "I've been calling you!"

"I'm sorry," I lazily responded, still searching, "I didn't hear you."

Mom's big brown eyes quickly shifted to the clothes trash mix scattered all over the place. I perked up attempting to take her attention away from my ram-sacked room.

"Well, I'm about to be on my way out," she started, "I won't be long I'm just going downtown."

She stood in my doorway momentarily scanning my cluttered floor with her nose turned up and a disgusted look upon her face. She made her way over piles of clutter to me and kissed my forehead. I was blinded looking at her pink pastel pants suit. Whatever is downtown, her curls might not make it. Mom's hair is so long they've already unraveled.

"Ok, I'll be leaving, soon."

"Wait, you know I need you to stay home today… the carrier might come by and I need you to bring in the package I been expecting, it's very important," my mother demanded, as she moved piles on my floor around with her feet.

"Okay," I replied, aimlessly looking around at my huge mess, "I'm missing out on too many days…I might have to repeat my entire freshman year."

"You'll be alright, Stacy, it's just one day damn!"

*Sigh* One day a week is more like it, if not more. I angrily tossed my uniform shirt onto my bed. Momma leaned in toward me with her hand perched upon her hip. She is really intimidating. Before she starts snatching me up, I started toward the other side of the room. I don't need her trying to rough me up this morning I'm still in shock over Sammy slapping Janessa. If my Dad were here with us she probably wouldn't need me to do silly things like this. Mom probably wouldn't be getting any packages at all. Especially, not from random guys or whoever she's getting all her fancy stuff from. Besides, if they really wanted to do something big they would put food in our house. Pointless, if you ask me, I want better for myself. Just because she didn't graduate that doesn't mean that I don't want to. I for sure don't want to wait around for packages all my life either.

"I just want to graduate with my friends on time," I began, "Can't they just leave the box on-,"

"Somebody can take it! You know that!" Mom snapped before trampling over my things toward the door then doubled back in an instance, "Clean up this filthy room! Is this how you like living?"

My mother left my room without another word and tightly slammed the door shut behind her. Relieved, I flopped down onto my comfortable bed and propped my aching body up against my green, plush pillows. An abundance of thoughts started to rush through my mind all at once. First, I wonder what she's getting sent over here now. Mom gets a package nearly every week from somebody and soon I'm just going to open one. Whatever the case, I have my own problems she's a whole other topic within itself. Besides, I was still thinking of last night. How could Sammy do that? I'm not going to school today, so I won't be able to check on Janessa until after three o'clock when she gets home.

The Thursday before spring break started, my cousin Dominic and Anthony had got into a fight in our homeroom class, literally right next to me! The two goliaths of the entire school were killing each other on top of me. That entire day seemed to be coming down on me, literally. I was sure it was mainly because I was going to be stuck inside my house for a week. Crazy, but I just couldn't shake the feeling of someone watching me. When I walked to the bus stop and down the street to my house; I felt something. Ever since that day, I imagined if I was a target and there was really someone out to get me. I try to view myself through a murderers' eye view. I'm not sure why exactly, just thinking outside of the box. Now, I chuckle at the paranoid thoughts. Why would someone be out to get me? I haven't been to sleep properly in weeks. I'm not sure of what is really my intuition or if it's just my mind playing a trick on me. Whatever, I just hope my mother left some money on the table.

I pouted for quite some time in my bed before making my way to the kitchen, hopeful. Although, I was really pissed at Mom I refuse to keep crying about every little thing she does to me. I stepped foot onto my trashy floor yet again then quickly made my way down the hall for a snack. Before the day had even begun I started to grow tired, too tired to do much of anything. I knew I was pregnant when my period didn't come two weeks ago at the beginning of the month and now March is almost over. I thought Sammy was going to ask me last night, especially after Terrell commented on my weight. I know he notices a change in me, too because I do.

After last month's mishap I figured that this was a possibility. Not to mention Sammy came to stay the night the week before last. I knew what I was doing, but now I don't know how I'm going to explain this to Mom? I peaked in the bare pantry and opened the mostly empty ice box. Nothing. Only last Fridays' leftover pizza and an opened can of grape soda. I shut the fridge door and opened the pantry doors again. Hoping that the food fairy had come by and slipped something in there while I wasn't watching. Luckily, Grandma Sarah kept me fed since there was no school this past week.

"Damn!" I yelled as I slammed the doors shut.

No matter how loud I scream or how much I beat myself up, the problem growing on the inside of me will continue to grow. *Sigh* There's no food and I'm starving like hell. I guess I really will be eating for two. All I can do now is sit down and think about what I'm going to do for this baby when I can't even do for myself. I dropped my head down on the table and wondered what my Dad would think or say if he was here.

"Damn," I realized, "How am I going to tell Sammy?"

My baby's father, Sammy, is seventeen and I'm barely fifteen years old. This is a curse I brought upon myself. It never even crossed my mind, the thought of me being pregnant, until the Friday morning that spring break started and I began to get sick. Damn, what am I going to do about my mother and this baby problem? I mean, how will I take care of it? I can't imagine walking down the street with a baby in one hand and all my dignity and pride in the other, gripping onto them both tightly. I glanced over at the clock on the wall and to my surprise nearly an hour had already passed by. I've been sitting at the kitchen table for quite a while. Lately, my mornings start off with me contemplating, it seems like that's all I ever do aside of try to get some sleep. Otherwise, I'm wishing I could be at school with Janessa and Dominic. Right about now, I would be in class with Janessa laughing about the fight my cousin got into week before last or how Sammy smacked the crap out of her. I would've seen my cousin Dominic in the hallways today and joked about the suspension that overlapped our spring break. Dominic is moms' twin sister Sherry's son and he's the only one that talks to us. I'm sure that's just because we go to school together. If we hadn't, I know for a fact I wouldn't know him as well as I do. The rest of our family thinks my mother is mentally unstable.

## (Doorbell Rings)

My thoughts were interrupted by the dramatic ringing. I quickly rose to my feet and rushed over to spy on my guest through the peephole. I reached for the knob and immediately realized that I had no pants on, only a tall t-shirt. I'm afraid that the carrier might leave if I try to go and grab my pants. I slightly opened the door enough for me to collect the box. I'm sure I look so silly trying to sign mom's name and grab the hefty package through the small crack. I know he seen my thin bare legs sticking out of my shirt. Though, the man respectfully kept his hat low over his eyes and paid me no mind.

"Have a good day," he said politely as he swiftly turned to walk away.

"You do the same, sir."

I shut the door, set the grubby box on the table and examined it for a label. Curiosity made me eager to open it I just want to know what it is and who sent it. It looks like the same package from the last guy. There was no return address with his name. I'm sure Mom doesn't need another pair of shoes. I shrugged my shoulders and went back to doing what I did best, just thinking. Before I nestled my bottom back into the kitchen chair the phone began ringing off the hook.

"Damn!" I said rushing to the phone, fanning myself with my hands, "Damn."

What am I going to do with myself? I know its Sammy calling, if not, then it's my Grandma Sarah. We never get any calls or visits from anyone. He also knows I rarely go to school thanks to Mom. If it's him I know he's going to ask me about last night or the possible baby and I don't even know what to tell him. I wish he would've just asked me last night, I mean, I'm not sure if I am pregnant or not I just keep getting sick, tired and hungry. I don't want to tell him yes and it might just be a cold or something. Then, I don't want to say no and down the road I am. I'll look like a liar or he won't believe it's his baby. I hope Sammy will understand the situation better than my mother would.

"Hello," I answered, my voice cracking under the pressure.

"What's up?" Sammy questioned, "You ran in the house yesterday…I just wanted to make sure you were okay."

Sammy's deep tone sent chills running through me. Those charming ways always send me swinging but, I could vibe that he was also nervous through the phone. I stretched the cord and paced the floor as we spoke.

"Are you mad at me?" He questioned.

"No, you didn't have to do that to her, though," I responded.

I continued to pace the floor as I chewed on my fingertips like a cannibal. Sammy cleared his throat before switching the topic.

"Have you been feeling okay, Stacy?"

"I'm fine, I've just been a little worried…you know."

"Yeah, I know where you're coming from, I've been a little worried myself," Sammy responded, exhaling deeply, "I just want to say if you're pregnant I'm sorry for everything and I love you with all my heart."

For a moment I was silent in amazement. I couldn't believe it. After a whole year of pretending to be so rough and tough I finally see his soft side, his true side.

"I love you, too," I replied with doubt.

"I want you to be mines forever," he expressed, "Even if you're not pregnant, I want you forever."

"I don't know, Sammy," I placed the phone over my heart for a second, "Let's just see what happens."

At this point, I didn't know what to say at all. We have been together for a little over a year now. I just can't see myself with him for the rest of my life. I can barely even trust him! I can't always reach him when I need him or want him for that matter. I'm too young and if I truly want happiness I can't be with Sammy. I need to grow up.

"Just trust me."

"I can't!" I exclaimed, "You barely even come around! I paged you all day yesterday and called your sister's house!"

"Come on please don't do this right now, Stacy."

"You waited until after midnight to come to get me, and you already had Janessa with you!"

"She came with Terrell," he responded.

"I honestly don't care, and I don't know what to do right now."

"Yeah, you do," Sammy expressed, "Be with me."

"I'm going to try and find something to eat I'll just talk to you later."

He didn't respond back to me, instead, Sammy sat in silence then hung up the phone in my face. I didn't know what else to say to him and I wasn't going to agree. Our relationship should end. I can't be fifteen years old with a baby and a whacky baby daddy! Just the thought makes me want to puke my guts. I sat back at the kitchen table and plopped my head down in my folded arms. Of course, if we were truly planning on getting "happily" married then it would be different. He will never make me happy. I guess I'll be like that girl Adriana at my school, although, she's already eight months. Luckily, for me, the school year is practically over. I pray that Sammy isn't going to be like those low life dads. Making up every excuse in the book of why and how they aren't the baby's father. I have yet to regret anything in my life, but this baby is one thing I think we can all agree on.

The night Sammy and I were first intimate I didn't necessarily want to do anything with him. He just kept asking and asking me until I finally gave in and agreed. Sammy and his play brother Terrell came to get me and Janessa from her house after midnight. Janessa's mom was sleeping, but I was so afraid that his noisy car was going to wake up the neighborhood. The whole time we were together, Janessa kept telling me how much she didn't like, Terrell. She thought he was too old, and she didn't let him anywhere near her. Unless he had some good smoke. Sammy took us to Terrell's where he and I disappeared into Terrell's room. I did not feel good about myself at all. I went directly to the bathroom to clean myself up. Before I could finish washing up Janessa barged into the bathroom with me. She looked really flustered and told me that Sammy tried to kiss her. Ever since that day, I felt like something was up between them. The four of us met originally in the high school parking lot last year around February. Sammy and Terrell assumed that Janessa and I were already of age. She pressured me into getting Terrell's pager number. But, Sammy wanted to talk to me instead, so I talked back. Going forward, Sammy has been in my face and on my nerves damn near every day. Janessa never touched Terrell and that made me feel worse. Now, I wish she had talked to Sammy instead of me. Until this very day, Janessa jokes that she should've got with Sammy instead. He's over-protective, though at the same time careless. After we were first intimate, he began to say crazy things to me anywhere from threatening to hurt me to telling me he loves me. I'm so confused. I know that he's capable of doing something that I can't forgive. He smacked Janessa's face so hard last night I got scared and I don't want him to do the same thing to me.

"Dear God, I know you have a plan," I prayed aloud.

Sammy isn't the greatest person, though he does make me think twice about dating any other dude. For the last two years Janessa and I have been getting into some sticky situations. We don't deal with the guys our age. Our motto is, 'eighteen and up,' because that's where the fun begins. Some days I can't reach Sammy and I hate it because he's never in one place. I find myself calling his sister Annette's house when he's not there he goes to Terrell's or to his Grandma Vicky's. Though, I forget about how angry or sad it makes me when I finally get to hear his voice on the other end of the phone.

By the time eleven o' clock rolled around, my thoughts consumed me. I began to wonder about my purpose on Earth. What does the good Lord have in store for me? It seems like the more I think the more I come to the same conclusion; nothing. Dad is locked up and I don't know anything about his family. Just my Grandma Marie, Dad's mom, she passed away when I was a kid and I don't know who my Dad's dad is, only that his name is William Viera. That's where we get our last name. As far as anyone else on my dad's side of the family, I have no clue. I wish we knew most of them, maybe then Mom and I would be better off. I stayed in the kitchen for nearly an hour more with my head down on the table and didn't eat a thing. I drank lots of water to curb the hunger until my appetite left. Eventually, I left with it and went back to bed disgusted. I took a nap hoping that it would help to ease my mind.

## Awake Again

By six o' clock that night I was up breaking out into cold sweats. I jumped out of bed whilst my head was spinning, my stomach was churning, and I was sweating bullets. I frantically searched for the lamp in my bedroom through the crippling darkness; I felt too sick to stand. I fell to my knees, crawled to the door and spit up all over the place just before I could get it open. The vomit splattered all over my wall and my junk filled floor. I was so afraid of what was happening to my body I rose to my feet and rushed to my mother's room down the hall. I had to go to the hospital, quick. When I finally reached her bedroom, I fidgeted for the knob quickly twisted it and rushed in.

"Momma, I need to-."

Although I was disgusted by the sight. I stood motionless in Mom's doorway.

"Stacy, baby please, it's not...it's nothing like that! It's nothing like that, hold on!"

The low life bum that lay in my mother's bed called out to me. I quickly turned away to run back into my bedroom and locked myself inside. The pounding from the other side of my door roared at me, demanding to come in.

"Stacy, open the door! Stacy baby girl, please open the door!" My mother yelled to me.

I held my cramping stomach tight and threw up once again uncontrollably in my trash can. Tears raced out of my eyes from the awful smell as I used my shirt to wipe my wet and reeking face. Moments later, the beating on my door began to die down. I sat in my pitch-black room on the floor gasping for air with my body propped up against the vomit drenched wall. The chattering on the other side of the door nearly slowed to a stop and it was something of a relief. A few minutes after the voices grew silent, the pounding on the door came to an end and the room grew even darker. I cautiously stood to my feet and wiped the aftershock tears from my slippery cheeks. My room was so crowded with filth. I crept over to the window and glared out the foggy glass to see if Sammy's car was still in the drive-way or parked along the street. I took off my slimy puke stained shirt, climbed into bed and laid there until the sun came shining through my window.

# A New Day

I woke up on top of my covers shivering, curled up in a fetal position. The sound of sizzling bacon and the awesome smell of actual food cooking got all my senses aroused. Since I missed school yesterday, I wasn't looking forward to going anymore and after last night I don't even want to look at, Terry. I could expect that type of behavior from Sammy, but my own mother? She was always the one telling me about her past and how much she despised Sammy because he reminds her of "those men." That's all I ever heard from her. Terry has always treated him like a door mat and Sammy has never really shown her much respect either. What so ever. It's been years since my Dad has been gone. Though, Terry claims she hasn't touched another man. She won't even bring it up! So, here I am. Once again, in my bed pouting, contemplating about that old wrinkled prune!

"She's been in there since last night…she's really upset with me, Mom."

"I know baby, she has every right to be I mean, Terry, how could you?" My Grandmother Sarah spoke.

I'd recognize that sweet soft voice from any distance anywhere around the world. Terry and Grandma Sarah must have been in there talking about last night for quite some time. They just kept going on and on about my father, Sammy, Aunty Sherry, and the summer that I will regret for the rest of my ever-changing life as long as I live here on mother Earth. Another thing I consider when it comes to regret. Though, I had more important things to worry about. Like what I was going to do with this baby. I mean, my baby. Gee, I hope it's a boy, I'm too afraid to have a girl. I'm so afraid she'll end up like me, a challenge full of sorrow and a disgrace. Fifteen and pregnant, not even sixteen or seventeen at least. I am fifteen years old and I am not getting an abortion. That I know for sure.

Oh man! I still can't believe it. I have to think about this. If I don't have this baby, then Sammy is out of my life forever! *Sigh* I rather have my child. There is nothing that bothers me more than abortions. Still, that would mean Sammy is a part of mine and my child's life. It would mean that every time I look in my child's face Sammy will be there staring right back at me. The very thought literally makes me sick to my stomach. I ran to the bathroom down the hall to relieve myself of morning sickness. I wonder why or how I got myself into this. Me! Pregnant!

"Stacy, sweetie, are you alright?" My mother asked rushing to aid me.

My mother's voice angered me. Before she could reach the bathroom I quickly kicked the door shut.

"Get away!" I said as I coughed, uncontrollably spewing out vomit.

"Stacy, baby…I'm only trying to help, please, baby I'm so sorry!" Terry pleaded in tears.

"Let your mama help you, child," Grandma Sarah demanded.

I came out of the bathroom the toilet flushing behind me. In the doorway,

I stood motionless angrily staring my mother and grandmother in the face.

"She can help me dig," I said sarcastically, breezing past them.

As if the hole I had dug for myself wasn't big enough. I slowly walked back to my room, sniffling. I wonder if she even suspects it, if the thought of me being pregnant by Sammy crosses her puny little mind. Next thing she says to me better be about a shovel. *Ugh* I'm not even hungry anymore.

# Pressured

Its July now. I moved in with my Grandma Sarah and I was finally happy. I found out that I was having a boy today! I wanted to tell my mother, but I haven't spoken to or seen her, for that matter, since early April. The only good thing about that is I'm finally sixteen and I found a job working at a restaurant downtown. I'm living my life and soon we won't need Terry or Sammy for anything. I've bought diapers, baby wipes, bottles, nipples and all kinds of essentials. I figured it's easier to be ready for my baby boy than to wait until he's born. I saved up over a thousand dollars so that eventually I can have my own place and be able to get a lot of much needed furniture. I really wish I could have a baby shower to invite my friends to and whatever family will come. Though, thanks to my mother I dropped out and haven't talked to any of my friends, Janessa either. I miss her more than anything. I'll probably never see my big cousin Dominic again, either. We're not that close to any of our family anyways. Hopefully, I can get a hold of Dominic I doubt that my aunt Sherry would even show up. Last year, was the last time I remember seeing my aunt. My aunt Sherry had my mother by the hair here in Grandma Sarah's kitchen. It was like watching a movie, you didn't know which twin was the good twin or which one was the bad one. I remember my mother picked up a knife everyone screamed, and Grandma pushed all the kids out of the way. Dominic and I joked about it this semester when we first found out we went to school together and had one class together. It's still funny, but I thank God my mother didn't hurt her. I still don't know what Terry did to make Aunty Sherry want to beat up on her so bad. Whatever the case, I'm going to make our lives better with or without family.

After tackling a little more baby shopping, I pampered myself. I did my hair I did my nails and got my feet done and stopped for a couple burgers before I got home. I felt like a woman instead of an irresponsible, pregnant little girl. When my swollen feet crossed the threshold that tub was calling my name. I scarfed down my food then sat in a warm bubble bath to sooth my back and muscles.

### (Doorbell Rings)

Who could it be? I angrily rose out of the suds and quickly ran into my bedroom to put on my fluffy robe. The bell rang three more times before I was able to make it back down the stairs and approach the door.

"Who is it?" I hollered.

No one answered. Cautious, I leaned against the door and asked once again, but still no answer. My legs grew weak as I tip-toed into the dining room. There was a snow globe from Grandma's glass table I picked up to use as a weapon. Slowly, I crept back over to the door to peek through the peep hole. Once I realized who it was I rolled my eyes and slapped my arms to my sides. I set the snow globe aside and reluctantly opened the door for Sammy.

"What the hell do you want?" I asked, angrily puzzled, "how did you find my Grandma's house?"

"Is that any way to talk to the father of your baby?" Sammy replied, smirking at me with that ugly, irresistible smile.

When he said that I knew he had been to see my mother. I never did tell him if I really was pregnant or not. I didn't want him to know. I was so disgusted I just stared at him for a few seconds before slamming the door in his face. Sammy is such a nuisance, he rang the doorbell constantly for about ten minutes straight. But, I ignored it. Eventually, he walked back to his car and sat in my drive-way for an additional thirty minutes or so. I didn't pay him any mind. Sammy realized he wasn't getting anywhere with me and drove away. At this point, I'm convinced that my mother must have told him where I was, for sure. I haven't talked to Sammy since that night I seen him in my mama's bed and it was very stressful moving away from home. I had a feeling he was going to show up somewhere at some point. I just can't believe he would show up here of all places.

For days now, I've been receiving multiple calls from Sammy at my Grandma's. Luckily, Grandma doesn't know yet. He was so desperate for attention he had his older sister, Annette.

"Hello."

I answered in a polite tone before I knew who it was. I didn't recognize the number on the caller ID just that they had called once before, but I purposely missed it.

"Hi, is Stacy there?"

As if I were trying to keep a low profile, I spoke in a soft voice.

"Yeah, this is she."

"Oh, well hey this is Sammy's sister, Annette," she proclaimed, "How are you?"

"Fine, how are you?" I responded, "How'd you get this number?"

"Good, and I asked Sammy to give it to me it's just nice to finally speak to you again," Annette began politely.

"It's good to speak with you again, too, Nette."

I placed the phone over my chest picked up the receiver and drug the cord with me over to the couch. I plopped down and prepared myself for the awkward conversation.

"I noticed my brother was a little upset today and I was wondering if you had any idea why?"

I thought it was so pathetic. Cute, but pathetic. Annette and I never even had a proper conversation because they always started off so awkward. It's like they hated to love me his whole family is crazy, just like him.

"No, not a clue."

Annette could hear the frustration in my vague response. I threw my hands up as if she could see me.

"Well, I think I know, I think he misses his love and I know he misses his baby."

Wow, no she didn't, the baby isn't even born. Why are these people so crazy? I'm sick of this already.

"I don't miss him, I don't need him, and I don't want him."

Slapping the phone down onto the receiver felt so good. What could they do for me? Get on my nerves. Be in my face. Neglect my baby. No, I don't think so. I'm truly shocked, how dare he try and have his sister call me? I mean, what was she going to do? I guess he believed that was going to help him get back in between my legs. Sammy had me feeling crazy, I was cursing up a storm and talking to myself. I felt like I was going to implode, I can't take dealing with him anymore. I also can't hide the fact that I still love him very dearly.

# Later That Day

It seems like Sammy has spent the entire week trying to get back with me and trying hard, too. I'm fed up with him I really don't want anything to do with him, at this point. I left it alone after I seen him in bed with my mother! Not to mention him trying to kiss up on Janessa a while back. I still can't wrap my mind around that! I had literally just walked out of his bedroom before Janessa barged in the bathroom on me. I should've known then he can't be trusted. From Grandma's dining room I had a clear view of the front of the house. For two hours or more I watched as Sammy drove back and forth past the house. I think he was driving past then, going to the pay phone to call. Then, get back in his car drive by before going back to the pay phone to call again. I'm so sure of it! Sammy called my Grandmothers' house about fifty more times before he got the picture and drove down the street erratically one last time. I just sat there with the snow globe and waited for my Grandmother to get home. Sammy drove by one last time just before Grandma walked in the door with a hand full of groceries. By the expression on her face I could tell that she needed my help.

"You should've pulled me outside Grandma I would have come to grab a few things."

"Oh no," she said, holding onto the bags tight and pulling them back from my grasp, "you go on somewhere and sit down."

"Grandma! Give me that bag, woman," I joked, as she slid right past me to the kitchen.

"Anyways, how was your day sweetheart?"

I sighed, "He showed up."

My Grandma whipped her head around to look at me, infuriated, "Here? Sammy, showed up to my house?"

I was too afraid to say anything stupid, so I just nodded my head and began to sulk hysterically.

"Mom, must've told him where I was, I haven't talked to anyone for weeks, Grandma."

She held me close and stroked my long, kinky hair as she patted my back. I really needed that from my Grandma, my mother never had time to hug me. I'm not truly surprised at her for sleeping around with Sammy. My mother doesn't care about me or anybody else, only herself. Terry's always getting expensive gifts and packages from some man I assume. Then, claims she hasn't touched anyone because she "loves" my Dad too much. I'm sure she slept with my Aunt Sherry's husband, Melvin, and I'm so sure that's why Sherry doesn't come around. What else could it be? My mom is so beautiful and mostly native. So, her hair naturally comes down to her waist line. Her appearance completely masks all the black in her from my Grandma Sarah and Grandpa Larry. God rest his soul. All my friends thought my mom was sexy with her slanted eyes like diamonds, brown fire skin like an original native. *Ugh* She makes me sick. I don't even know the whole family history, aside from that I wonder how her relationship was with my Dad.

"She's probably still sleeping around with him and he's like seventeen, Grandma," I cried.

Grandma Sarah let me go and felt no remorse for me. I wiped my tears and began to help her put away the groceries. Grandma Sarah suddenly stopped to turn to me again and paused. I felt Grandma about to tear me a new one, in so many words.

"You shouldn't have been with that boy no way. I don't know what's wrong with you and your mother. Letting you run the streets just like she did! Except you don't have to lie to do what you want to do."

She stood in the middle of the kitchen with her hands on her hips and her head hung low. Grandma was in deep thought. Suddenly, she glided over to the knives and snatched up the biggest one.

"Hide this under the cushion of the couch," she directed, "If he comes over here again I'm going to have to hide him, you hear me?"

"Ma'am," I responded with doubt, though, I took a hold of the butcher's knife.

Of course, I would never try to stab Sammy or even pretend just to scare him. I don't care what he does to me. Grandma made her way to the dining room and without another word I followed behind her. She nestled into the love seat as I planted the knife under the sofa cushion of the larger couch. She leaned her head back on the rest and began to sulk.

"I should have been better," Grandma said covering her face slightly, "I knew what she was out there doing."

I rushed to my Grandma's side, dropped down to my knees and held her just as she held me. We've cried together before, but I had never seen my Grandma breakdown so hard. I remember when my Grandpa Larry passed away she didn't cry then either, she called it a celebration of life. Now here we are living, pain free and she's crying like I've never seen before.

"Nobody is blaming you, Grandma," I said, gazing into her beautiful brown eyes.

"Nobody's around to point the finger," she profoundly wept, "Hell, Sherry don't come around... she won't answer the phone and she leaps around town so much I can't get her address."

My heart damn near skipped a beat. I was just thinking of my Aunt Sherry and Dominic, too, I miss him the most.

"I know what, Terry, was out there doing and your damn daddy did, too!"

I rested my head in Grandma Sarah's lap and listened closely. My mom always talked about how much of a good man my Dad was. She never told me things to paint him or her out to look like bad people.

"But mom says he was a good-"

"Charles...your Dad...was a dog, and he trained your mama like one, too," she interrupted, "He beat her down until she knew exactly what to say and do."

"She never said that," I replied in awe as Grandma stroked my hair.

"She's not going to tell the truth...she's always been a habitual liar. A lie! Just a damn lie! That's all the child did was lie!"

I couldn't stop crying as I peered into Grandma Sarah's tired eyes. I didn't want what she was saying about Dad to be the truth, but I understand Grandma's deep frustration. She loves my mother so much, but mom's behavior has become intolerable, even for me. Grandma's telling me without telling me Mom used to hit the streets. I'm not sure and I don't want to be.

"I wasn't there for her, Stacy," she searched the ground for answers after taking a long pause, "Someone hurt your mother...and I will forever blame myself for the way she is."

My jaw dropped! "Those men" she always talked about were real. Instantly, my mind attempted to travel back in my mother's life and empathize for her. I know exactly how it feels to be taken advantage of. I smacked both hands against my face to force the tears away and silence my thoughts. Though, as my Grandmother continued to weep aloud the emotions burst through my lips. A long cry from deep inside my gut left my mouth and sorrow wrapped my heart.

"I wasn't there for her...and we weren't there for you," she began to wipe a few of her tears, "She was only fourteen and she was fast!"

Just like me! I placed a hand over my quivering lips to once again hold back my tears as I repeatedly shook my head in disbelief. My mother is an angry person, now I guess I understand the reason why.

Especially, after what happened to me at that party last summer. Although, the relationship I had with Sammy upset her, I'll never understand the reason why she slept with him. I wish he would've never crossed my path. Sometimes I wish that my mother wouldn't have brought me into this crazy world at all.

"I don't know what really happened, but I know one of Larry's friends touched my daughter...and it hurts me...she didn't even tell me when it was happening to her."

Grandma Sarah stared off into the distance for a while and shook her head in disappointment.

"I love you, Grandma, you have to let mom go... she's not a little girl anymore," I pleaded, "You can't stress yourself over the past it's not healthy, I had to get away from her too she's never going to change!"

"It wasn't her fault," she started, "What happened to you wasn't your fault, either."

My heart erupted in my chest. Now, Grandma's comparing my situation to Mom's. It couldn't have been as bad as what happened to me.

"I don't want to talk about that, Grandma," I expressed, "There's never any food in the house she's always gone, and I had to drop out of school because of her!"

Grandma Sarah began to cry hysterically. What can I say to put her at ease? I continued to hold back my tears and strayed off the topic of me. It wasn't about me right now. Besides, I felt bad for my Grandma and I still wanted to smack my mother. It was hard to feel remorse for her. Terry seems to be at the bottom of every problem plaguing my family. The little family that we have, our extended family members refuse to interact with any of us. Grandma Sarah is an only child and none of my Grandpa's family like my mom very much. My Grandfathers' surviving siblings and their children, most of my cousins, have no respect for us.

"I was so happy when your father went to prison," she instantly stopped crying, "There was no stopping him…I'm surprised your mama is working now! All that damn money they had."

Money? I'm sure she means the money that mom would have if she were still with my Dad. I'm sure my mom isn't getting big bucks and I know for sure she doesn't have a job. My mother can't even keep food in the fridge. She is either downtown or waiting around on a package.

"What money, Grandma?" I questioned curiously, "What did my Dad really do?"

She gazed at me as if I had asked her the ultimate questions. Grandma thrust herself back against the couch once again and chuckled inside of her throat with her eyes closed. She rested her head in her palm then momentarily paused before responding.

"Well, Charles…honey, your mother should really be the one to tell you all this and I say that because-" again, she sat up slowly considering whether she should say certain things to me, "Hell, he killed some man your mama was probably messing around with…killed him in cold blood."

Grandma placed a hand over her forehead and took a deep breath before sulking, "Be better than your mother, Stacy and be better than me, baby!"

I nodded my head in agreement, though I had no idea what she fully meant. Dad's a killer? He killed a man over my mother and now I can't see him. *Ugh*

My mother is such a hand full. How is it that she causes so much hurt and pain, but still wants the love and respect? What I did come to find out is that my mother is running the streets doing something. Right now, it's Sammy. Whatever her and my Dad had going on didn't just affect my life. Grandma Sarah abruptly got up from the couch and started back into the kitchen.

"Help me put away the rest of these groceries, baby," she quickly switched the subject, "Have you eaten yet?"

"No," I replied following her into the kitchen, "I'm starving."

Romance filled the living room around midnight as I watched late night television, still dwelling on everything Grandma had said earlier. Of course, my mother wasn't going to tell the truth she's probably too ashamed. Everything Grandma had said about my Dad got me thinking about what kind of man he really was. Mom never mentioned that he was a murderer she always said that he was a good man and nothing less. I'd like to think that he didn't really beat up on my mom. Yet, if Dad is a murderer then that cuts even deeper. My mother was probably afraid of him, aside of that, I've never known my mother to be one to deal with pain. I remember she went to the hospital because one of the many packages she gets almost every week dropped on her foot, she is that dramatic. Sigh I continued to stuff my face with Grandma's mashed potatoes. I was happy to see her get some much-needed rest. It was an eventful day for the both of us. Kind of makes me wonder what my mother is doing now.

## (Knock, Knock)

My thoughts were immediately interrupted by an unwanted guest. I picked myself up off the couch and dragged over to the door.

"Who is it?" I asked politely.

"Sammy," he responded confidently.

*Sigh* I rolled my eyes then opened the door to gladly curse him out. I twisted the knob and pulled the door back to reveal a belligerent drunk, wobbling back and forth ready to fall down the two short steps. I crossed my arms over my bulging belly and stood back.

"What are you doing here?"

"I'm waiting for you to tell me to come inside," he responded near perfectly clear.

"Leave," I told him, "Now."

When I reached to shut the door, Sammy snatched up a good grip of my long, dark hair and jerked me outside. We stumbled over the threshold and out into the cold rain. I had on no shoes, pajama shorts and a short shirt that fit snug over my growing belly.

"Let me go!" I yelled throwing punches up over my head as hard as I could, only a few hits connecting in anonymous places, "MY STOMACH!"

Sammy flung me around by my ponytail wildly. He finally let my hair go and let me stand toe to toe with him just before he smacked my face. I backed away and put my hands up in self-defense. Sammy rushed toward me again and nudged me down onto the ground. I splashed into a puddle of cold, dirty water that soaked through my thin clothes.

"Why do you want to fight?" He questioned, out of breath.

I glared up at him from the gravel with a blank stare. I couldn't say anything I was speechless. Sammy got really flared up, reached down to grab me by my shirt collar and snatched me up off the ground. I assume the neighbors are entertained or just ignoring the situation. Across the street there was a big park with a soccer field and a play set but it's too dark and rainy for kids to be over there playing. No one can save me from his deadly grip on my throat, cutting off my air supply so swiftly. As Sammy punched me in my sides it grew increasingly more difficult for me to breathe. All I could do was take it. I fell helplessly to the ground once again. Only this time, a white four door car sped down my block. The drunken idiot must've thought it was a police officer, stopped kicking my ass, ran away and raced off in his car.

"Thank you, God," I prayed from the dirty ground peering up at the sky.

I was so afraid! For a few seconds I was paralyzed on the gravel. The rain fell hard and fast, peleting my entire body. I imagined Sammy turning the car around and coming back to try and run me over. All the strength that I had left I used to pick myself up and drag back inside to my bed. That was a blessing, I think he was really trying to hurt me...to hurt us.

# Anguish

I woke up the next morning curled up on my bed. My palms still raw and bleeding a bit, my legs scratched up and my clothes were riddled with dirt from the puddles of mucky water. I got up to use the bathroom and look in the mirror, though my legs were barely working for me. There was so much pain in my back I could hardly breathe. I stood in the bathroom mirror disgusted. Silently I cried to myself and lay on the cold, damp floor. My shirt lifted just enough for me to press my aching back against the ice-cold tiles.

"Why, why, why?" I whimpered.

My heart filled with hatred, anger, hurt and so many more emotions all at once. My stomach knotted as I wept to myself trying not to wake my Grandma. Hopefully, she didn't hear anything last night. Sammy was snatching me around so much that crying or calling out for help barely came to mind. Eventually, I picked myself up off the floor and returned to my bed with the same dirty, disgusting clothes.

### (Knock, Knock)

"Stacy, are you awake?"

My Grandmother questioned as she allowed herself into my bedroom. She crept in over to my window and drew the curtains back. I sniffled as I tried to hide the tears falling from my swollen eyes.

"Good morning, Grandma," I groaned as I sat up in my bed.

"Are you okay, baby?" she questioned, "What's wrong?"

Grandma Sarah rubbed my left cheek then pushed my bang back to reveal my right eye. She could see a dark bruise nearly blanketing my beautiful brown shade. I pushed the covers back to once again drag myself out of bed. Grandma's jaw dropped in awe. I revealed to her my arms, back and legs riddled in cuts and bruises.

She turned her head and closed her eyes tightly, "Did he do this to you?"

"Yes."

My Grandmother quickly dropped her face in the palms of her hands and sobbed. I painfully sat down on the bed next to her and hung my head low in shame. She turned to me and wrapped her arms around me tight. For a moment, it felt like she was never going to let me go. I honestly was waiting for her to curse me out and call me stupid or something for opening the door.

"Why'd you open the door?" She finally questioned.

"I don't know, Grandma."

"This is why I told you to hide the knife!" She hollered, "Why didn't you use it?"

She pulled back away from me and dashed over to my closet. Grandma tore through my clothes found me something to wear and forced me into it my clothes.

"Come on," she urged, trying to hold herself together, "We got to go to the hospital."

"No!" I refused, "He'll go to jail."

"Yes, he will!"

I can't do that to Sammy. He's just mad because I don't want to be with him anymore. Sammy's sick and no one understands him. He may need a lot of things, but jail is not one of them. He's only seventeen. I sat back down on the edge of my bed and sulked.

"Grandma, please, he's just sick he needs help," I pleaded, "Not jail."

"We have to check on the baby, child, don't you understand?"

"He didn't hit me in the stomach," I confessed, "Only my back and legs hurt, I'm just soar."

My Grandma placed her hands on her hips and let out a deep sigh. I know she's worried about the baby, I am too. Except the little aches in my back, I feel just fine. She stood silent and stared at me from across the room. Without another word she flung out the door and slammed it shut behind her.

# December

Whispers of my mother's voice slipped into my dreams waking me up out of my sleep. I opened my eyes, I wasn't dreaming she was here. Sigh I lazily threw the sheets back and carefully got out of bed to head down to the kitchen. My mother sat at the table with my Grandmother watching as I slowly scooted to the fridge.

"Hey, Stacy," she said happily, "You're getting big, girl."

The sound of her voice was so annoying to me, I stared her down gritting my teeth. Terry sat quiet in dismay, then scoffed at me.

"I'm trying to speak to you little girl," my mother snapped.

Still, I ignored her as I rummaged through the cupboards in search of hot tea packets. My mother got more and more angry, but I know that she knows exactly what the problem is.

"Look at here," my mother began.

"Look, Terry," I barked back, "Don't speak to me unless spoken to."

She leaped out of her seat and attempted to make her way over to me. I whipped around and snatched a knife from out the holder.

"Don't touch me!"

"I dare you to stab me, bitch!"

My Grandmother stood between us and began to push my mother back towards the front door. I stood there ready, wielding the knife in one hand and holding my stomach with the other. Suddenly, I started to feel excruciating aches in my sides. I doubled over and fell to one knee as the pains grew stronger. The blade fell from my hand to the tile floor missing my foot by just a few centimeters.

"Grandma! Help!" I yelled.

What seemed like urine spewed down my legs and drenched my pajama bottoms. All eyes stared at the puddle on the floor beneath me.

"Help! I'm peeing!" I cried.

"Terry!" My Grandmother called out.

My mother leaped into action. She pushed past Grandma Sarah grabbed the phone and called the ambulance. Terry hung up the phone and dashed to my room to grab sweat pants and a light jacket to get me ready to go.

"Mom!" I screamed in terror, "Mom! Help me, please!"

"Momma's here," she assured me, "Momma's here I'm not leaving you, baby."

Grandma Sarah helped my mother drag me into the front dining room as the ambulance arrived in no time. This day couldn't have come soon enough. I allowed Terry to come with us to the hospital given the circumstance. I wonder why she was at Grandma's this morning to begin with. Otherwise, Grandma would have gone to her house. Honestly, I'm just glad that she was there.

### (Ambulance Sirens)

"It's okay sweetie, take deep breathes everything is alright." My Grandma Sarah coaxed.

"It's finally happening," I told her.

My stomach cramped and contracted so terribly I anticipated on the epidural shot. That way I can get through this pain without literally passing out from shock. Gee, I imagined I would be in pain, but I didn't think it would be like this. The doctors know what to do, but I'm so afraid of pushing him out of me. I feel like something out of a creepy alien flick. One where the monster comes bursting out of someone's poop shoot. At least that's the way it feels, like my baby boy is pushing everything inside of me down and out of my body all together.

"Dear Lord, please let him be okay," I prayed, "Give me the strength to birth a healthy child."

# Day Two

I sat up in my two-day old aroma in the hospital bed. No wonderful child in my arms. Not a smile on my face, just dead silence and the occasional sound of a beeping monitor. It's almost like I wanted this to happen in a good way, of course. I wined as I tossed myself back on my pillows, my hands and arms thrown over my head. *Sigh* I had to do it. After the fight, I never went to the doctor I knew they would've asked me about the bruises on my four month long pregnant stomach. Grandma Sarah is still a little upset with me about it, too, but I couldn't throw Sammy under the bus. He's not the monster they would have painted him out to be. Sammy's just mad right now because I don't want to be with him. I can't have him do to this baby what he does to me, so, I hope this adoption is a good choice. It's not that I don't want him, I didn't want my baby to be afraid of Sammy like I am. Afraid of what's going to happen or what's not going to. At least the baby can be somebody and away from Sammy. He must've felt that I would do something drastic like this. He hasn't tried to come around since he kicked my ass.

### (Knock, Knock-Squeaking Door)

"Stacy? Stacy is you up?"

I heard Sammy's annoying voice conspicuously enter the room. I slowly sat up and watched as he snaked over to me. He's not dressed like a gangster today. It is Sunday. Though, I was happy to see the flowers. Sammy should button his shirt and tuck it in every day.

"How you feel? You need something?"

Dumbfounded, all I could do was look at him not a word left my lips. It really astounds me the way he acts like he has done nothing wrong. Sammy stood in the middle of the floor unsure of what to do with himself. I could tell when the silence was beginning to be too much for him.

"You're not perfect either, you know," he finally said as he locked eyes with me.

Here we go, I was wondering when he was going to flip the script on me and start acting. Like he's trying to get nominated for an award, but I'm the only one in the audience patiently waiting for the show to be over. Sammy is so up and down. It's hard to tell when he's being genuine or when he's trying to manipulate me into doing what he wants. By telling me what I want to hear just to turn around and do the total opposite. He's got to be the sneakiest person I have ever known. I can't wait until the day that he leaves my sight for good.

"I don't mind your flaws, but when it comes down to me, I feel like I'm walking on eggshells," Sammy declared.

Tears began to crowd my eyes. If I ask him to leave the room he'll probably do something stupid like snatch out the IV in my arm. Sigh I never win these bottomless arguments. Mainly because he's always looking for a specific answer that I don't have for him. Sammy is such a bad liar. He doesn't think at all before he speaks, it seems. There is no reasoning with him. Either he is right or you're wrong. There is no in between. Before I parted my lips to speak to him I thought long and hard about what I should say.

"I don't understand life yet...and I'm scared of what might happen next with you around."

I couldn't help it. I broke down for the first time since the doctor took my baby boy from my arms. The nurse warned me that constantly holding my baby would only make me want him back. I took her advice and detached myself from him mentally and emotionally. As soon as I realized that I would never see him again I wanted him back. Sammy placed the beautiful bouquet of flowers at my feet and sat up on my bed side.

"I understand why you did what you did, Stacy."

He grabbed a hold of my hand and kissed it repeatedly as a lonely tear rolled down his cheek. Was this the break through? Did I just see Sammy have an epiphany? I mean, now he knows I'm serious I gave our baby away.

"Please, let me love you better...I can, I can love you better, please," he begged.

I leaned back against my pillows, gazing into Sammy's eyes. My hand softly gripped in his palm.

"I don't know, Sammy, I have to-"

Before I could finish my sentence, he quickly arose from my bed side. Sammy tossed my hand into the air and stormed out of the room. I watched as he shut the door behind him. I can never understand why he doesn't just let me finish what I have to say before he gets upset. I hope he walks out of that door and never walks back into my life.

## Lost Love

The hospital released me to my Grandma Sarah. It was around ten o'clock, I lay in my bed asleep without a thought on my mind and I dreamed of beautiful things. It almost seemed as if I were awake, though I was sleeping. I could hear footsteps and my bedroom door tightly closing shut.

"Stacy. Stacy, get up."

The deep, whispering voice sent chills down my spine. My eyes slowly opened as I tried to make out the dark figure that stood before me. I gasped in shock.

"What are you doing?"

Did Sammy just break into my Grandma's house? I thought I was done with all this at the hospital, but now he's gone too far. As I babbled and stuttered trying to find the words, I thought to myself, 'how in the hell did he get in here? Why is he here?'

"Hush, girl!"

Sammy suddenly paused and began to pace back and forth across my bedroom floor.

"Did you break in here, fool?"

"I don't know what to do, Stacy, I already apologized," he stated, "I apologized a hundred times!"

"Sammy!" I shouted.

"What do you want me to say, Stacy? Huh?"

I was so afraid and puzzled with nothing more to say. I thought maybe my Grandma let him in, but she doesn't even like him. Surely, he didn't hurt her and got inside. He may be crazy, but I don't think he's stupid. She seemed terribly serious about stabbing him if he comes back. Now, here he is.

"Stacy...do you want to leave me? Just tell me now."

I didn't respond, he practically knew that we were done before I was six months pregnant. Way back when he fought me, and I was totally sure that he got the picture before I left the hospital today. After all, he did leave first with an attitude. I was expecting him to do something outlandish while we were at the hospital. Now, I kind of wish that he had, I'm so damn scared my body is shaking like a leaf.

"Answer me!" He silently barked through his teeth at me in the darkness.

Please don't hit me, please don't hit me, I thought as Sammy crept over and slowly seated himself next to me. I was nearly off the edge of my bed while still scooting back to get away from him. I finally fall off, once the back of his hand slid across my cheek. No shock, it just frightened me more. Like any other time, I was more afraid of the pain. I held my beat red, heated cheek in my shaken palm. But, I didn't cry. Instead, I jumped to my feet and ran for the door before Sammy caught me by my hair. I was barely clutching the knob then I flung back into his arms.

"Calm down," he said with his hand tight over my mouth, "Don't go running out on me."

I wriggled away from his fatal grasp and swung back violently. Sammy tussled with me until he was finally able to hold my arms in his tight grip once again.

"Leave me alone! I don't want to be with you, I don't want you in my life anymore…you wore out your welcome."

Sammy frowned; his head hung low as a tear fell from his eye. I cried with him and leaned into his sweaty chest.

"Man, Stacy damn! It wasn't supposed to-" and for the first time Sammy sobbed which seemingly convinced me, "Don't let it end like this."

Careful, I pushed myself back away from him.

"What are you talking about?" I wondered, "Something is wrong with you."

"I'm talking about us, Stacy," Sammy declared, gripping my forearms tight.

I shook my head in disbelief as I watched him fall to his knees.

"I'm tired of you hurting me," I cried, "You don't have to do that to me."

Sammy jerked his neck back and his nose turned up toward me.

"I don't believe in us anymore than you do. You

don't hurt the people you love," I continued as my eyes filled with tears.

"Stacy," he pleaded.

"No! you never cared about me or the baby," I told him.

Sammy abruptly stood to his feet."

WHAT!" He yelled.

"You're acting like you care now because I gave him away…you tried to kill my baby," I said with tears streaming down my face.

He began to go plum crazy punching holes in walls and throwing my things all about. Something is mentally wrong with Sammy. For real.

"That's why I gave him away," I sulked crouched down at my bedside, "So he wouldn't have to deal with you! Now, get away from me!"

Sammy stopped for a short while. He looked ugly crying.

"You didn't let me see him, Stacy," Sammy sulked, "I didn't get a chance to hold him."

"I don't care! Get out!"

"How could you say that? You don't mean that, Stacy."


**(Knock, knock)**

I gasped, "Grandma."

"Stacy," my grandmother called out.

From the other side of the door she tried twisting the knob. But, it was locked.

"What's going on in there? Open this door, Stacy!" She demanded banging on the door.

When I reached for the handle, Sammy reached for me, "Wait."

"Please, my Grandma," I declared beginning to cry.

Sammy snatched my hand away from the knob. He pushed me aside and opened the bedroom door.

"Sammy? Stacy? What are you all doing in here?" My grandmother asked confused, "How'd you get in here? Stacy, how did he get in here?"

The room had been trashed. Sammy tossed my clothes, my baby's clothes and moved my bed clear across the floor. Before Grandma Sarah could step foot inside Sammy began to shoo her out and block the horrid view.

"Come on Grandma, I'll take you back to your room," he volunteered.

"You shouldn't be here, son, it's too late," she told him, "What was all that noise, Stacy?"

"The television set was on, Grandma," I responded.

Sammy awkwardly stood in the doorway between me and my Grandma Sarah. Luckily, the hall light was too dim to reveal the havoc in my room. He was determined to get grandma back to her bed quickly.

"Let me take you back to bed before I go home," Sammy offered as he pushed past her, "I'm just checking on, Stacy."

"It's okay, Grandma," I assured her.

"Okay," she said from down the hall, "Goodnight, baby."

After a few minutes, my Grandma finally went back to bed. She didn't too much care for him and I know she knew that something was wrong. Sammy came back to the room with his hands in his pockets and his head still hung low. I sat at the foot of my bed, still rubbing my swollen cheek. He cautiously came over to me and wrapped me up in his arms just like a baby, he cradled me in his lap.

"Stacy," he called out to me with a shaken voice, "I'm sorry, I am so sorry...I love you, Stacy."

Sammy held my arms up desperately attempting to force me to hug him back. Every inch of my body was numb. Snot ran down my face as tears filled my eyes. I put the last bit of trust into Sammy that I had left. Warn out tired and absorbed by fear, I shut my eyes and fell fast asleep in his arms.

He rocked us back and forth, "Just trust me, Stacy...don't leave."

# Valentine's Day 1988

Since my decision, Sammy's gotten better with his attitude. Of course, many times I ask myself, why is he still a part of my life? Honestly, I've never been with anyone else. Not seriously. I wouldn't even know how to be. From time to time Sammy will rough me up. Just like my mother, but other than that he's good when he's good. After the beatings, the screaming, all the arguing and fussing or fighting, then we're fine. I end up with an angel in my arms or holding me tight massaging the bruises away. Although, I'm sure he's running around on me I'm not worried. Now that Sammy knows that if it weren't for this baby we're having now, I'd be gone. I know for a definite fact he dreads the very thought of me living happily without him. While on the other hand he would be lost without me. We've been engaged for seven months now. I know because I'm only seven months into my pregnancy and for the moment I'm happy with life.

Sammy and I moved closer to downtown in East Denver, our neighborhood is scenic and from our two-story townhome we can see the tall buildings in the inner city. Sammy works downtown as the manager of a department store and I work as a secretary at a small business close to our home. Having this baby won't be anything like my first pregnancy, giving up my child was the hardest part. Sammy was the sole reason why I did it, but I can't continue to blame him for how I feel. I shouldn't have been with him to begin with. Sigh The only way to go from here is forward I don't want to keep holding on to what happened in the past. Then, I'll never be happy. All I want to do is work hard and go home to my family.

"So, what are you thinking about doing for your man tonight?" Tracy asked out of curiosity.

Tracy was a good friend of mine. We were both full time secretaries for the small business. I'm forced to share a desk with this wild one for eight hours a day and five days out of the week. We ended up getting acquainted so well because our names sounded so much alike. She's been a very good friend to me and I've told her about most of the things I've been through in life.

"Ha, nothing at all," I replied with a smirk.

"Mm. Girl, you're a mess!" she laughed.

She broke out into an annoying laughter and as serious as I was Tracy didn't believe me. With a blank expression I looked over to her then fiddled around with my band.

"I'm serious, Stace," Tracy said, playful pushing me to the side.

"I don't know, Tracy, girl…I get way too tired."

Tracy smiled, "You will be just fine."

"You think so?"

"Girl, yes!" she replied, "Me and my man are going to see a movie, eat and then go to his place!"

Tracy bounced her shoulders around and snapped her fingers with joy. I couldn't as get excited.

"Oh, that sounds good, where are you going to eat at?"

"Girl, I don't know he better not be lying to me again," she spat angrily.

"You are too much!" I laughed, "I'm sure he's taking you some place nice or else its curtains for him."

"I'll shove all the damn curtains down his throat!" Tracy idiotically replied.

We were interrupted by the door swinging open and a handsome man coming into the office. As he made his way toward the desk I grew increasingly anxious. 'I know this man!' I thought to myself. Tracy crossed one leg over the other and rested her chin in her palm. The man locked eyes with me and a warm smile stretched across his face. Jet black hair braided down his back and a light complexion, like mine.

"Stacy? Do you remember me?" The man questioned curiously.

"Dominic!"

My cousin, Dominic, could see the exhilaration by the way I sprouted out of my chair and clung onto his buff neck. I haven't seen my cousin in three long years he's changed so much I barely recognized him.

"Cousin, how have you been?"

"I've been good," He began, "looks to me like you're doing okay, too."

"I am," I told him, "Dominic, this is Tracy. Tracy, this is my big cousin, Dom."

Tracy happily stood to her feet pulled her shirt down over her bottom then stretched out her hand, "Nice to meet you."

"Likewise," Dominic said with a wink.

"What are you doing here?" I questioned.

"Me and moms was talking about you," he explained, "I started asking around and here I am."

"Well, I'm going to be leaving work around four o'clock," I expressed, "Tracy was taking me to eat while she does happy hour. Did you want to join us?"

"Yeah, we need to catch up," Dominic said.

"Great! Meet us back here at four and we'll go from there."

"Here's my pager number just in case your plans change," he confessed, "I'll see you at four."

After a great day at work, Tracy and I waited for my cousin Dominic to arrive. He patiently waited outside for us both.

"I'll take you wherever you want to go," Dominic began, "Then, I'll bring you back to your car."

"I don't mind," Tracy was quick to respond, "I'll take you home, Stacy, you know that."

"Perfect! Let's head to Franklin and get a catfish dinner."

"Sounds good to me," Dominic expressed.

We arrived at our destination in no time. The three of us were so eager to get inside we didn't give the other patrons a chance to get out. Once inside and ready to eat Dominic kept Tracy and I laughing. I almost forgot how it felt to laugh so hard and for so long. We stayed for nearly two hours until I realized it was starting to get dark out.

"It's starting to get late," I began, "My man is going to get worried."

"I'm sure he would've paged you by now," Tracy added.

"Nope," I responded, checking my pager screen.

"If you're ready I can get you ladies back to the car," Dominic said.

"Yeah, please."

"Check!" Tracy called out across the room.

Dominic locked eyes with Tracy, they shared an awkward chuckle.

"You are so ghetto," I laughed.

"It's cute."

"Don't egg her on."

Dominic got us back to the office just before the sun kissed the horizon. Tracy drove me home while still convincing me to do something for Sammy. Since it was such a beautiful day, I started to consider it. I was so happy to have seen my cousin I didn't care what happened. Nothing was going to bring me down. We pulled into my complex and immediately my closest neighbor across the way from me waved us down. I wonder what she's going to tell me today. This has become routine, I mean, I get off work to come home and Sharon's beating me to the door. She lives just across the way in the complex closest to mine. Since the day we moved in, she sits up on her perch like a hawk looming over the people down below. Sharon has a scarf for every occasion. She's always smoking that same cigarette.

"Tracy, do you mind pulling over, so I can get out here?" I questioned politely, "That's my neighbor, Sharon."

"Yeah," Tracy pulled in as I watched my neighbor back out of the exit to park next to me.

"Have a goodnight!" I exclaimed making my way over to Sharon.

"Hey, Stacy, you just getting off of work?" She asked.

"Girl, yes about to get in here and eat," I expressed.

"Well, I hate to be the bearer of bad news, but I saw a woman over your place earlier," Sharon began, "Tall, light-skinned skinny thang."

"How long was she in there?" I asked.

"I'll tell you what, she walked in there with her weave up and came out with it down," Sharon explained.

"Okay, thank you for letting me know, Sharon."

Sharon nodded her head and slowly pulled away. I started toward my place with no emotions. Honestly, Sammy is never going to change, and I'm threw trying to force him. My head was held high only to have the very uplifting feeling knocked out of me once I stepped foot in the door. Sammy smacked my face and erased every happy thought I had flowing in my mind.

"Did I deserve that?" I said with my head tilted and my face still stinging.

"Where have you been? I've been sitting here for an hour waiting on you!"

I lifted my heavy purse from my shoulder and

tossed it to the ground. Then, took two solid steps toward him ready to fight.

"An hour?" I asked, my teeth clinched, "I sit up damn near every night...one o'clock, two o'clock, three or four in the morning!"

"I'm talking about today, where did-,"

"I'm talking!" I interrupted, lunging at Sammy.

My anger shined over the fear I felt as my lips quivered. Sammy snatched his neck back in amazement.

"And, Sharon told me you had her over here again," I confessed, "I know it's, Janessa."

We locked eyes and the expression on his face told me everything that needed to be said, had been. It seems as if my old friend Janessa and I have been in the same relationship all this time. I wonder how good he treats her, I thought stomping away. I'm not going to allow him to stress me and my baby.

"I was talking to you," he shouted, "Stacy!"

I walked up the stairs to my bedroom flipping him the bird all the way. Once I shut my door and locked it I could hear him knocking over chairs and breaking glass. Until he finally grabbed his car keys, got the hell out and slammed the damn door behind him. Typical, he screws around with the girl and gets mad at me because I told him to his face. I can expect that from Sammy, after all, Janessa isn't the first and I know she won't be the last.

# Restless Night

Sammy came home trashed. *Ugh* the nerve of him, bringing his loud-mouthed homeboys home with him after midnight. Now, I can't necessarily get up and go to Grandma Sarah's. He would get in the car and bring me back home anyways, but at least his friends would be gone. They all sat in the living room drinking and smoking out my place like a chimney.

"Sammy! Sammy, baby!" I screamed down the stairs politely.

In front for our friends I put up a front because he respects me enough not to rough me up when they're around. Sammy slowly came up to the room and stood in the doorway sloppy drunk.

"What you want, girl?"

"Can you shut them the hell up! I'm up here trying

to sleep!" I scolded, "You should've went somewhere else."

Sammy took a deep breath as he quietly came in, turned to slowly shut the door behind him and inched toward me.

"You know what," he began.

I tossed back the covers and jumped out of the bed ready to fight with him. In the darkness we stood face to face.

"What? Tell me something…because if I lose this one, you lose me…that's it no more chances," I threatened.

I waited for him to react with a slap or a punch, "whatever you want to do I'm ready for you!"

Sammy was in awe, "But, Stacy, I-,"

"Shut up! Get out of my room, get out of my face! Go!" I said pushing him out the door and slamming it behind him.

Ten minutes later there was complete silence. Sammy slowly crept back into the room to grab a pillow and a cover, then left again to sleep on the couch. Suddenly, I felt like the bad guy, but loves not supposed to hurt and it's time for him to feel my pain. I'm ready for a change and now that the tables are turning he's going to have to change to or get rolled over.

Around four o'clock that morning I woke up wrapped in Sammy's arms, to my surprise. I looked back at him and there were two big brown eyes peering through the darkness back at me. Sammy kissed my forehead and pulled me in closer.

"I'm sorry I love you, Stace."

For a moment I stayed silent holding back the tears until I finally responded, "It's okay."

He kissed my cheeks and my forehead again then held on to me tighter, messaging my round belly. If he still doesn't realize it, then I guess I've got to. No matter what happens or has happened we both have to keep in mind that we're bringing another child into this world. Before we damage another life, we need to deal with our problems together.

# Confrontation

My eyes opened to the sun shining bright in my face as early as it seemed, Sammy was already gone. He must have left last night while I was sleeping. Before I got the chance to properly stretch someone was beating on my door. I slowly peeled back the warm blankets and crept out of bed. By the time I had stood to my aching feet the person had knocked at the door over five times, banging hard, too. The closer I got to the door the angrier I got. Constant banging persisted as I quickly snatched the chain lock, unlocked the door and snatched it open.

"Why the hell are you beating my damn door down?" I barked, shocked to see Janessa standing on the other side.

"Where is he at?" She snapped back, attempting to push past me.

With all my might, I placed my hands against her chest and shoved her out of the doorway. She generically stumbled backward and tripped over the stair. Luckily, she landed on her bottom and didn't hurt herself too bad.

"Oh, hell no!" Janessa exclaimed, quickly standing to her feet ready to pounce.

I stepped outside of my apartment with my fists tightly balled up ready to fly. I watched as Janessa repulsed and attempted to grab me by my long ponytail. She clawed and scratched at my face as I threw punches at her stomach and sides as hard as I could. Janessa was so tall and lanky that she was able to overpower me just a little.

"Let her go," Sharon yelled from her balcony, "She's pregnant."

"Let my hair go," I warned Janessa.

"Where is he at, Stacy?" She yelled, holding on to my hair tight and punching at my face.

Honestly, I wondered why she wanted Sammy or why she was even here this early to begin with. She pushed me back and quickly bound backward down the single stair and onto the grass. The neighbors began to step outside to try and take us apart. Though, I continued to charge at her now that she had already got me out here looking crazy. When I stepped to her again she attempted to throw her hands up and quit.

"Stop, Stacy, you're pregnant!" Janessa said, devilishly smiling in my face.

"She's pregnant stop!" Sharon screamed from her balcony, "I'm calling the police!"

I punched her in the stomach, grabbed her top ponytail and punched her face until her nose gushed with blood. Once again, Janessa reached up, grabbed hold of my ponytail and pulled me down into the grass with her. Those long, lanky arms pulled me underneath her body weight as Janessa sat upon me.

"Watch my stomach," I told her as I punched at her face and neck up over my head.

Screeching tires and loud music broke up the crowd. The next thing I know, Sammy came to the rescue. He and Terrell pushed through the people to yank Janessa off top of me.

"What are you doing here?" Sammy screamed at her, "She's pregnant!"

"Leave now!" I screamed as I began to throw punches at him, too.

Terrell picked me up and dragged me in the house, "Stop! Get the hell off me!"

I yelled, kicked and screamed as I wriggled out of Terrell's grip to run back to my bedroom. I took Sammy's clothes out of the closet along with his shoes and one by one threw them out onto the front lawn. Many of our neighbors are outside watching in amazement and I don't care what they think. I took his gold chains off the dresser and tossed them out the door, too. Real fourteen karat gold.

"You better come get all your stuff," I demanded, watching him scramble to collect his things.

"Stacy!" He called out to me before looking to Janessa in disgust, "Get out of here!"

Janessa pleaded for Sammy to come with her instead, "I'm sorry, just come home."

"I am home!" He stated, pushing her away, "Are you stupid?"

Blood was dripping from her crooked nose and

dried up around her face. The more she wiped her tears the more she smeared the blood onto her cheeks and in her hair. Sammy was sickened by her. He once again pushed her aside and continued to collect his things. Terrell stood by his belongings looking on to make sure that no one grabbed anything while he was searching for his gold chains. I came to the door with another arm full of Dickies pants and white tees watching as Janessa pitifully cried her heart out to Sammy. Holding together her torn up blouse.

"He doesn't care about me," I shouted from the door, "So, he really doesn't care about you!"

Sammy turned back to look at me as I gleefully tossed his belongings out onto the grass. Janessa flipped me the bird on both hands, then slowly backed away to return to her car. Without a second glance at Janessa, Sammy rushed toward me. I hurried to shut the door and lock it before he could come inside.

"Get away from my damn door," I shouted, "You can get the rest of your stuff when I throw it out tomorrow."

He calmly knocked on the door, "Stacy, open the door."

"Bro, watch out!" Terrell shouted to Sammy.

Janessa drove her car up onto the sidewalk, onto the grass and finally up onto the porch of our front door. I could hear people screaming and the sound of a car engine blaring. Before I could peek out the window I heard a loud thud on the door. I quickly snatched it open only to be faced with Janessa's bumper.

"SAMMY!" I shouted.

I thought she had already hit him, but I guess

it was just his body slamming up against the door. Sammy fell inside and with all my might I dragged him in as he kicked his feet to scramble inside with me. We trembled in fear as Janessa backed her car up then revved up onto the porch again. She was crazy. But, she couldn't kill Sammy she only wanted to scare him.

"Terrell!" He screamed as he rapidly stood to his feet.

Sammy stood in the door way worried that his brother might be hurt, luckily, Terrell jumped off to the side like everyone else did. Terrell scrambled to get inside with us as Janessa was backing out. She almost hit some people in the crowd around our complex. Janessa sped away from my building and was immediately stopped by police officers blocking the exit. The people stood outside of our complex talking to officers and giving them the story before we were able to say anything at all. A single officer came to the door and spoke to me about what further action they had planned on taking. Once I told him that I didn't want to press charges he offered to take me to the hospital to check on my baby. Though, I refused. I felt fine, though I knew Janessa needed a doctor to check out that honker. I turned the officer away and shut the door a final time.

"Sammy," I started, still facing the door with my head hung low and my hands on my hips.

He didn't say a word. Sammy rushed over to me and held on to me tight. The anger I felt toward him completely went away. All I could think of was what if she revved all the way up on to the door and killed him. I turned around to face him and wrapped my arms around his neck as he rubbed my belly.

"I'm so sorry," he began.

"Look at me."

I pulled away from him to look him in his eyes, so he knew I was serious. There was something that I needed to say to him. I'm trying so hard to say anything at all. Inside I'm screaming, 'I love you! You're alive! I'm sorry! Everything is okay!'

"Come here," he said, pulling me in close.

Sammy already knew what I was trying to say. He gazed into my eyes and seen what I saw, too. The bumper of that old, beat-up duce and a quarter. I didn't have to say a thing. She was swinging her momma's boat all over the sidewalk and up in the grass. Never put anything past anybody. Up until today, I would've never thought Janessa could do something so crazy. I'm glad she really does love Sammy or else she would've killed him right there.

"I love you so much, I'm so sorry," Sammy whispered to me, "Never again."

"I love you, too."

We stood there for well over half an hour, I held on to him tighter and tighter every minute. Terrell gathered up the rest of Sammy's things outside and brought them back in. Just before leaving, he hugged us both for a few moments and cried, too.

## April 1988

My mother stood at my bed side with my tightly clinched fist in her palm, "push baby, your almost there!"

I panted and pushed, pushed and panted. Finally, out came the baby.

"It's a boy!" my mother smiled.

I was so relieved to have passed that one. Then came another pain, and I started to push and pant once again.

"It's crowning, Stacy I need you to give me another big push," the doctor urged.

I cried out to my mother, "Mom, help me," as I pushed at the same time.

Out came the other. I was cleaned up and sewn back together, still Sammy was nowhere to be found.

At the last minute, he came bursting into the room sweating profoundly and trying to catch his breath.

"Stacy, baby, I was trying to get here as fast as I-," he paused as a smile stretched across his face.

"Twins!" he said happily.

He rushed to the bed and scooped up one of the babies. Sammy smiled uncontrollably as our baby boys cried and cried. I could hear the low buzz of his pager, though he ignored it.

"Did you already choose names, Stace?" he asked, hoping that I hadn't.

"No, I was waiting on you, babe."

Sammy smiled happily, "Chane."

Once again, his pager started to buzz, and once again he ignored it. I didn't think anything of it.

"I'm not good with names...what about Corey," I said.

My mother and grandmother sat together with joyful tears, "beautiful babies, precious, precious little things," my grandmother muttered.

Sammy stayed at the hospital with me. Ever since he arrived his pager has been going off. Every now and then he'd glance to see who it was but, he didn't make any calls. I was up all night by the time Sammy had got up around one or two o'clock in the morning. Convinced that I was asleep, he used the phone to return a call and slithered over to the window with the receiver. I watched as he glanced over at me to check if I was up or not.

"Hello," he waited for a response, "Yeah, my bad my pager dropped in Terrell's car."

Why, am I not surprised? Phone calls at booty call hour had Sammy written all over it. His so-called brother, Terrell is every girlfriend or baby mama's worst cheating, lying nightmare, too.

"My sister was having her baby, so I had to hurry up and go or else I would've stayed a little longer," Sammy said without a break.

I gasped. One, I contradicted myself I thought that there was really nothing else that he could do to surprise me. Two, I fell for him once again, I felt as if blades were piercing me through the heart, though I didn't say a word or make a noise. I had to hear what else he was going to say to, obviously, what seemed to be another woman.

"Feel bad for what?" he questioned then sat quietly for a moment.

What should I do about him? For the past couple months, since Janessa nearly killed him, he's really changed a lot. He started to come home at night more often instead of not at all. At least he's paying the bills, but when Sammy's with me he might as well be somewhere else.

"Nessa," he said trying to interrupt her, "Janessa, don't worry about it, alright."

At this point I have truly had enough I'm literally dying on the inside. How could he still want her after everything that she did? I startled Sammy with my wailing. He whipped around to find me sitting up in the bed groaning in rage. Janessa was my best friend. She's the whole reason why I'm in this Sammy mess to begin with. For goodness sakes, she tried to kill him.

Sammy slapped the phone down on the receiver and rushed over to me, "Stacy! Damn."

"Get away from me," I told him, "No! Don't touch me...ugh, you disgust me!"

After struggling to get out of bed I limped over to my clothes. Slouched over myself, I made it down the long hallways as nurses tried to tell me to get back into bed. I paged my cousin Dominic then used the front desk phone to call him.

He answered the phone mumbling and yawning, "Talk to me."

"Dom," I cried, "I need you to come and pick me up from the hospital please, cousin."

"Which one?" he asked frantically.

"Downtown on Bannock," I said as I burst into tears, "please, it's kind of cold and I have my kids."

"Stay where you at, I'm on my way."

I snatched up my babies and walked out of the hospital. Moments later, I could see Dominic recklessly pull into the pick-up lane. He noticed me standing on the curb with a baby under each arm and Sammy blocking my way. Dominic quickly raced over to me and pushed him aside. Cousin grabbed for Corey took me by the hand and walked me back to the car.

Sammy chased behind us, "Hell no! Stacy, get out of the damn car!"

Dominic slammed the passenger door behind him then turned to throw a punch as Sammy threw one back. I sat in the car with my eyes tightly shut. It hurt me to see Dominic pulverize Sammy. Bludgeoning each other until Sammy was just too exhausted. Once the fight was over Dominic got in the car and quickly sped away.

"What happened?" he asked furiously.

"He's been cheating on me with, Janessa," I said trying to hold back the tears.

"Janessa?" Dominic took a deep breath, "Do you need to go home and get anything before stupid gets there?"

"Yes, thank you again, D," he glanced over at me shaking his head in disappointment.

We got to my place and there was no sign of Sammy's car in the parking lot. Dominic held both of my babies as we walked up to the door. Inside, it was dark and reeked of weed and cigarettes. I grabbed everything that I could for the babies and for myself. We rapidly stuffed the car seats in the back of the car and buckled the boys in. I went back inside as Dominic sat in the car with the boys waiting on me. I made sure to grab the key that I had incautiously left behind. Slowly and painfully, I scurried out the door back to the vehicle as Sammy raced around the corner and down the street. He quickly bound out of his car and rushed over to me. Sammy grabbed my arms and began shaking me hastily.

"Don't leave, Stacy!"

Dominic swiftly snatched my soar body from Sammy's grasp.

"Get in the car!" My cousin demanded.

"No, Stacy, you already home just come in the house, come on," Sammy coaxed as he held his hand out to me.

"I'm tired of you hurting me," I spoke with pain in my face as tears fell from my blood red eyes.

Dominic watched as I shook my head in disappointment and turned away to get back in the car. Sammy lunged at me before he was overpowered by my cousin. Once again, they brawled in the front yard. Dominic fatally beat him then got back in the car to take me and my children to his apartment in the far northeast.

"You can stay with me as long as you need to, okay," Dominic told me, heavily breathing.

It's been a week since I left the hospital. I've gotten a million pages from Sammy. My mother has paged me every moment of each day. Every time I call her house she starts complaining about him coming by at weird hours of the night asking where I was. Sammy has been consistently stalking my mother about where Dominic lives. He's left voicemails on my work phone demanding that I come home with his kids. Eventually, the job the I was proud to have fired me. Sammy mentioned my name during his rampage, on the hunt for me. Hoping that I would show up to work in the mornings. I have yet to get the proper amount of sleep. I haven't been to sleep for more than three hours without my pager buzzing, or my babies crying. It doesn't really matter to me whether I sleep or not, so long as I have my angels I'm okay. Since the first morning here with Dominic, I've routinely gotten up taken care of my twins' needs and then my own. I shower, wash out my clothes from the day before and then cook whatever was available for me to put together. There is nothing like home, except that every day here feels better than home. My cousin got up stretching and yawning on his way into the kitchen.

"What's that?" he grumbled, wiping the sleep from his eyes.

"Breakfast," I informed him, "I just put potatoes, with eggs and crumbled bacon over it with some onion I chopped up in there."

"Thank you, cousin," Dominic said,

He retreated to the sofa with the condiments. I watched in disgust as he doused it with ketchup. *Ugh* I can't stomach the way he eats. Even though, I don't have much room to speak. I have had worse, like lettuce and ranch every night for weeks at a time. Dominic reached beneath the couch for his shoebox top. He rolled a joint and took a few puffs before devouring his bowl.

"Do you smoke?" He questioned.

I didn't say yes, but I wasn't going to say no. Besides, I wasn't breast feeding and I needed a little stress to be relieved. I seated myself on the couch with him and puffed his joint.

"All this time I've been here I haven't asked you anything about Aunt Sherry, where is she?" I questioned, anxious to know.

"Mm, she's around," he began, "She don't like being in this area."

"It's not too bad if you stay inside," I joked.

Dominic glanced over at me and chuckled then back down at the shoebox as he scraped up another joint to roll. I started to feel bubbly, light headed and giggly.

"Are you sure you smoke, Stacy?"

"No," I responded bursting into laughter, "I never smoked in my life."

Dominic watched as I teeter-tottered next to him on the couch cracking up. At first, his face expression was as stone and he seemed very serious. Though, after hearing my infectious laughter he couldn't help but to laugh with me.

"You are crazy, dude," he told me, "Where's your mama?"

I passed him the joint back and coughed uncontrollably for a moment. Fanning myself with both hands, struggling to breathe.

"She's around," I said sarcastically, then broke out into annoying laughter.

"You can't hit this anymore," he laughed.

"No," I giggled, "I can't."

My face began to turn a little red as my beat red eyes bulged. I laughed so hard that I couldn't breathe for a second. I had to stop my thoughts completely and hold my stomach as I took in several deep breaths.

"Okay," I said sitting up-right and wiping away the tears of joy.

"Okay," Dominic laughed, "You sure?"

My stomach cramped, and my cheeks grew soar after laughing so hard for so long.

"Yes," I started, "But, um, seriously though I was living with Grandma Sarah before I moved with Sammy."

His face twisted up, "Why?"

"She slept with Sammy."

"With Sammy?" He asked flabbergasted.

When I spoke about it out loud I sounded so stupid to myself. When I say yes, I hope he doesn't say anything to make me feel worse than I already do. The whole situation is shoddy to begin with.

"Wow," Dominic expressed, "You must really love him."

"What do you mean?"

"You chose him over your own," he told me, "Or, not?"

I didn't know how to respond. Sammy is usually the one to leave me feeling speechless.

"No, she chose."

"That's what I wanted to say, but I won't put your Mom out there like that," Dominic said with ease, "That's disrespectful."

"Did she really have sex with, Melvin?"

He quickly locked eyes with me as he rapidly gestured no with his head, "Never that."

"Oh, then, what did she do?" I asked eager to know, "Why did Aunty Sherry fight Mom in Grandma's kitchen?"

Dominic finished rolling the second joint and sparked it up. He deeply inhaled, harboring the marijuana smoke inside his lungs before releasing it. A large cloud of thick weed smoke filled the air.

"She was trying to get my Dad killed."

I didn't want to say that I didn't believe him, but I just didn't believe that my Mom could kill anybody. Or, want someone else's life to be taken from them especially, not with family. I paused momentarily watching him take long pulls of the joint. My jaw was dropped, and I almost didn't want to ask him anything more.

"Why?"

Dominic stood to his feet, shaking off marijuana crumbs onto the floor. He put the shoebox back underneath the couch and nestled into the sofa pillows.

"My mom said, Terry, was stealing money from, Charles," Dominic started, "When your Dad caught her she lied and told him that my Dad never brought him his money."

"My dad, Charles?"

Dominic looked over to me confused with an eyebrow raised and slowly nodded his head, yes.

"Charles came to my house, slapped my Mom around and was about to shoot my dad."

"...Did he?"

Dominic frowned and without a word he answered, "No, he had your Mom with him."

I'm floored I wonder how he knows all of this. What if he was telling a lie that one of our other disrespectful cousins told him? Just because they don't like my mother and they don't want anyone else to like or love her either.

"How do you know?"

"I was watching from the closet," he responded, "When I heard my mom screaming I got scared, thinking my Dad was going to whoop me next...so, I hid in the closet."

"What did he do?" I pressed, "What did you see?"

"Charles put the gun in my dad's mouth and asked Terry again if he never brought the money... my mom was screaming at her to tell the truth, but she was scared."

"My mom took the money and your dad got killed over that?"

"No! He didn't kill him," Dominic shouted, "Terry told the truth then your dad turned around and hit her so hard she fell on the ground and didn't make a noise."

"My dad knocked out my Mom?" I questioned, astounded.

"Yup, picked her up and walked out my house."

Why is it that I'm just now finding out about all

these different things? My mother never told me anything honestly. She said that Dad was a good man. He's starting to sound like a monster.

"Was your dad okay?"

"Yeah," he responded, "My mom was so mad she never looked at Terry the same."

"Not at all," I agreed, "I wouldn't have known what to do."

"Mom, she didn't know she almost lost my dad," Dominic wiped his sweaty forehead, "Charles was going to kill my dad with one word all it took was for Terry to say yes."

Sounds to me like mom was a Bonnie and dad was a Clyde. Lock, stock and barrel the two of them together. It's frightening that I don't know at all who they are. Truthfully, they don't know me either. The feeling of not knowing is starting to be a comfortable place for me. Dominic sat up for hours watching television, playing with the babies and smoking. I fell fast asleep.

"I'm about to make moves, Stace, get up," he confessed, "I'll bring back some diapers for the babies."

"Okay, they look like this."

My twins slept gracefully as I leaped over them and into the back room. I brought out a box of tiny diapers.

"That won't last for the month."

"No, it won't," I responded, "I'll pay you back as soon as I can."

"Don't worry about it," he told me before leaving out the door.

# Midnight

Dominic barged into the apartment and went directly to his room. He came back out to the living room with a chrome pistol. Or 'Sick 'Em,' as he called it.

"Dom, what's going on?" I asked franticly.

"This fool is outside," he responded, focused on filling the clip of his gun, "I'm about to kill him."

I scooped up Corey and Chane then placed my boys in the back room and ran out to stop Dominic from facing life in prison, or worse. When I stepped foot out the door, I found myself amid a barrage of flying bullets. Trembling, I ducked beside a neighbor's car until the shots ceased. When I finally opened my eyes, my stomach was numb my body grew cold and weak. It seemed like water running down my legs. Once I glanced down, I seen nothing but red covering my clothes and my hands. Shocked, I dropped to my knees spewing blood from my gut as I wondered how I didn't even feel the bullet hit me. I could hear Dominic's voice faintly screaming my name in the distance before I blacked out. Sammy reached me before Dominic could. He quickly scooped up my motionless body, tossed me in the back of their car and rushed me off to the hospital. Sammy cradled my motionless body in his arms while at the same time shooting out the window at my cousin. Dominic chased the car a few feet before stopping. He remembered leaving us upstairs in his apartment.

"The twins!" he said frantically turning back, "Damn!"

He got back up to the apartment and noticed the door was wide open. Dominic raced to the back room only to find my boys were also gone.

"Damn!" He yelled, dropping to the floor hopelessly.

# The Last Day

L uckily, I decided not to breast feed my babies, so Dominic was able to care for them while I've been in the hospital. I remember Sammy's blurry face in my vision as he whispered soft spoken words in my ear, rocking us back and forth. I could barely hear a thing or say a word. Although, I vaguely remember feeling pints of my own blood dripping down my sides. I don't remember getting in or out of the car. I am in total shock! Contemplating how I ended up in the same hospital for a different reason. A beautiful nurse came into the room with a clipboard and a smile, interrupting my thoughts. The way she poked around the bed checking the wires and pushing buttons on my monitor let me know she was here while I was sleeping. Of course, but where the hell is Sammy? He's going to miss his cue. Besides, I'm confident that the twins are still with Dominic.

"Hello, my name is Kimberly I'm your nurse," she began, still poking around the monitor.

I didn't respond I just lay in the bed afraid to move and watching her closely. Nothing makes since to me anymore. As soon as this woman gets out, I'm snatching out this damn cord and I'm going straight to the payphone.

"Mr. Jacobs, your fiancé, brought you in two nights ago unconscious," doubtful, the nurse pressed on, "Do you have any idea how this might have happened to you?"

"I don't remember," I responded politely.

I couldn't say anything about what happened. That would mean Sammy's freedom, not only that but Dominic's freedom, too. Over something that I could have prevented. All I had to do was go inside the house when Sammy asked me to. Then, my cousin wouldn't have fought him, and I wouldn't have gotten shot.

"Okay, well, there will be some medications given to you to take for the pain," I nodded to her in agreement, "Was there anything else? Did you have any questions?"

"No, thank you," I replied still puzzled about what happened to my cousin, Dominic.

She wrote a few things down on her clipboard and made sure that my colostomy bag wasn't too full. Kimberly softly grabbed me by the wrist and stretched out my arm.

"We'll go ahead and get you some more medicine to keep the pain away," she happily expressed, "sound good?"

No wonder I wasn't pissing in the bed. I don't remember getting up to pee at all. It's like I'm in the twilight zone. I'm not completely in the dark, but I have yet to see the light. Kimberly stole awkward glances every now and then before she left the room. The nurse stood in the doorway and I can tell there was so much more she was supposed to get out of me.

"Oh, an officer is going to be in soon to ask you a couple more questions."

"That's fine," I said energetically.

Maybe now I can get out of this mess and home with Dominic and my kids. All the cop wants to do is ask me some questions that I won't have any answers for. Nurse Kim returned moments later with my medication. Along with her came Sammy and his parasitic brother, Terrell.

"Here's your family!"

"Thank you," I replied with my eyes locked on Sammy.

"Okay, well ma'am, if you need anything, I'm just a buzz away."

The guppy nurse left the room with a smile and tightly shut the door behind her. Sammy's confident eyes locked onto mine.

"The doctor said you'll be alright, but you need to stay at home...in the bed."

Disgusted, I picked up the phone on the side of my bed and began to dial Dominic's number. Sammy snatched the phone out of my hand and slammed it down on the receiver.

"I'm not going home with you my cousin has my kids!" I said with confidence.

Terrell chuckled beneath his breath as Sammy softly smiled, "Your cousin has my kids, really?"

He looked to Terrell then back to me with a devilish smile. Terrell stepped out into the hallway.

"What did you tell them, Sammy?"

Sammy placed both hands in his jean pockets and stood firmly in the middle of the room. The brim of his hat hid the smirk on his face.

"I told them we were out and about, then someone started shooting."

"Don't lie to me."

"Just don't say too much," he chuckled, "Dominic will be under fire if you do."

Before I could respond, the door slowly crept open. A familiar, older woman with slightly gray hair came inside. She was holding my babies tight under each arm as she walked over to Sammy then gave Corey and Chane to him.

"Grandma V, do you remember my beautiful wife and the mother of my children?" He happily pointed to me, "Baby, Grandma Vicky."

"It's nice to finally meet you," Vicky smiled, totally clueless, "A little thing like you had to carry those babies."

I'm under the impression that Ms. Vicky thinks I'm in here because I just had my babies, which I did. Now, I feel like I'm going nuts and anger is consuming me. Once again, I have fallen victim to Sammy and there is nothing that I can do about it. I lay back in my hospital bed with no emotion on my face and no feeling in my heart. I'm hopeless, helpless, scared and I'm in dire need of someone's help. I watched as Vicky and Terrell left the room with my boys. Remembering that the nurse said an officer was coming in to talk to me, so I got an idea.

"That's okay," I said sitting back up to devilishly smile in Sammy's face, "A cop is coming to talk to me, I'm just going to tell him."

"Tell him what?" Sammy pressed, "You kidnapped our kids from the hospital and took them out into the cold, went to the house grabbed everything, but food for them then went to a dope spot with your cousin…which by the way tried to kill me and shot you instead."

I propped up against my pillows and accepted the checkmate. Damn, I didn't think that through, he's right. Sammy always wins! Now, I know this isn't going to go the way I want. I can't risk getting my cousin locked up for only trying to help me. I should have never pulled him in to this. Sammy stood to his feet and came over to my bedside.

"Just get some sleep," he planted a kiss on my forehead then turned to leave the room, "We'll be home soon."

### (Knock, Knock)

"Come in," I told the unwanted guest.

"Denver Police," the officer announced as he entered the room, "Ms. Reyes, ma'am."

"Yes, sir."

Sammy calmly sat on the other side of the room pretending to be unafraid. He rested his ankle upon his knee and leaned back in his seat.

"I'm officer Fields," he told me, "How are you doing?"

"My eyes are open so, I can't complain."

The officer glared over his shoulder at Sammy looking really unsuspicious. Then, extended his hand to greet him.

"Hello, sir," the cop started, "Officer Fields."

"Charmed."

"I understand you personally brought her in night before last?"

Sammy sat up properly, "Yes, sir, this is my wife."

"You want to start by telling me what happened?" Officer Murray turned his attention.

"We were going out for a night on the town and shots rang out all around us," he lied, "I couldn't tell where they were coming from."

"And, where were you all when these shots were fired?"

"Close to Peoria there's a club," Sammy told the officer, "But, I really don't remember where."

"There are usually a lot of strange happenings in that area," Officer Murray confessed, "No place for a young family."

"No, sir," Sammy angrily agreed.

Officer Fields wrote a couple things down in his note pad and gave me his card.

"I have your address here, call if you have any more information."

Officer Fields mistook my gloomy attitude for something else. Of course, he assumed that I was still in shock from being shot. He turned his attention back to Sammy.

"Looks like she's going to be, okay, for now," He expressed, "She's lucky to have you."

Sammy stood to his feet and started towards the door with him.

"Thank you, sir."

When Office Murray left the room a piece of my sanity left with him. I tossed the card across the room and carefully rolled over onto my side.

## Summer 1989

It's been a year since I last heard from Dominic. I haven't been able to go by his house because Sammy usually has the car and takes me everywhere that I need to go. He won't even allow me to go to work anymore. When Tracy realized I was fired she tried coming by and calling the house, but Sammy warned me not to talk to anyone. I'm trapped under his rule, watching our kids and cleaning constantly. I can't sleep I feel so unhappy I cry myself through every day. No laughter, I never smile anymore unless I have my babies with me or I've finally gotten away from Sammy. Even when it's only for a few brief minutes I'm always happy to get away from the likes of him. The twins, Corey and Chane, are one entire year old and they count on only me for everything. Sammy is often too busy and out partying most of the time, it's like the only parent they know is me.

Every morning that this summer has brought starts off with an uplifting song. This morning, I felt like taking the shackles off my feet, and believe you me, I was surely dancing. It was nine o'clock and the day can't get any better than this. *Waaah!* Poor child of mine, either Corey or Chane is the first one up and the first one crying. I quickly made my way to the bottom of the staircase and too my surprise, both of my beautiful boys were wide awake. My crybaby is Corey, he always wants to be held. Chane, that's my little tough guy which at times scares me because I don't want him to be like his daddy. They were each at the top of the stairs afraid to grow wings and slide down on their bottoms. I made my way halfway up the flight to help them down.

"Slide down on your bottom, Chane."

When Corey sees Chane doing things he tends to follow suit. In order to teach them, I show Chane and in return he teaches his brother.

"Corey, it's okay, sit down on your bottom, baby."

This time around Corey got up the courage to turn on his stomach and slide down toward me. I was amazed! I clapped my hands and congratulated him as I secured my footing and scooped him up in my arms.

"I'm so proud of you!" I said kissing his chubby cheeks, "Come on, Chane."

Chane stood at the top of the stairs in shock. It seemed to me like he was standing up there scratching his head, wondering how on Earth Corey learned to slide down himself.

"Let's go get your brother," I laughed making my way up the rest of the staircase.

Chane hollered at me, I assume he's saying no.

My precious baby quickly turned on his stomach and slid down the stairs toward us. We all giggled as I cautiously stepped backward down the stairs gripping Corey and the railing tight. Chane slid down further and further each stair I stepped down from until we reached the bottom floor. I set Corey down as Chane crawled behind me to the living room. We clustered in the middle of the room and danced around the coffee table. The music was so loud we didn't hear Sammy opening the front door, but we heard him slam it.

"Daddy!" My boys jumped for joy.

He trudged right past them without a second look and cut the music.

"Why is the music so damn loud?" He yelled in my face.

I didn't say a thing. I just wiped his spit from my eye and guided the twins into the kitchen. Whenever Sammy gets loud with me in front of my boys I let him fire, it's better than looking stupid with him. Instead, I look stupid around him. No matter whether we argue or not I'm always the one left looking crazy in the end. I sat the boys in their high chairs and slopped some hot creamy wheat cereal in their bowels.

"You in here getting fat?" Sammy yelled from the living room.

*Ugh* I thought it was just me. I'm stuck in the house so often I'm starting to blow up like a balloon. I glanced back at the boys making a mess in their high chairs. They each glared back at me, giggling.

"You hear me?" Sammy pressed.

I whirled around, crossed the kitchen and stood at the sink pretending to wash dishes as I cut my eyes at him. In the sink there was a dirty butcher's knife I used to cut through a slab of ribs last night. I'm never the one to press the issue though I will be the one to make a damn good point.

"I'm talking to you!" Sammy barked as he inched his way toward me.

"I hear you," I responded sarcastically.

"I'm gone all day then when I come back you have an attitude," he announced, "What are you doing behind my back?"

I didn't respond to his silly question, obviously I'm right here where he leaves me every day with the kids. Finally, he got sick of the awkward silence and began to swiftly make his way into the kitchen. Before the twins could see what Sammy was about to try and do to me. I snatched up the knife and charged toward him with it.

"Hey!" Sammy yelled before he bolted in the other direction, "Stace!"

Before he made it to the front door I stopped short and I watched in amusement as he reached for the knob. While Sammy fumbled with the lock I backed away to show him that my intentions are not to physically harm him. He stole a few glances back at me then stopped trying to escape.

"Why you got the knife, baby?"

"I love you," I responded as I tossed the knife aside and held my hands high for him to see, "I won't hurt you, leave now."

He felt that I was inviting him in and came to me, "Baby, I'm-,"

"No, just get out of here," I barked, "You don't love us."

Sammy ignored my request and dawdled toward me again for comfort. In an instance, I gestured as if I was going to pick up the knife. Sammy dodged out of the front door. Before returning to the twins I locked the door and picked up the dirty knife. My boys were in the kitchen still eating as if nothing was unusual. They looked to me and giggled with their beautiful gummy smiles. I think the twins thought that Sammy and I were just playing a game, which is good. I washed the knife off and placed it in the dish strainer then cut the music back on.

Sammy returned home around one o'clock in the morning, it was the earliest I had seen him home in the past few months. He ran up the stairs and into our room timid, drenched in sweat and heavily breathing. As if the squeak of the door wasn't loud enough, the minute I heard him breathing I was conscious. He tip-toed over to my side of the bed, sat near me and rested his hand on my back. At first, I was hesitant to sit up though I glared at him as he sat there peering through the darkness at me. The moonlight shinned brilliantly through our mesh curtains, making his silhouette appear to me perfectly. I could make out his rich chocolate skin, beautifully illuminated by the moonlight.

"Sammy," I called out.

He jumped back in fear, "Baby, why are you up?"

"What are you doing?" I paused responding with a question, "What's going on?"

Sammy sat before me on the edge of the bed still gripping my waist in his sweaty and shaken palms. I sat up to wipe the sweat from his brow as he squeezed me tight.

"Stacy, do you love me?" he asked suspiciously.

"I do, baby, why are-,"

"You told me I didn't love you...you said I didn't love my boys," he interrupted.

"You don't act like it," I snapped, glaring deep into his moonlit eyes through the dark.

"I love you..." Sammy started to choke up on his words, "...and I love my kids."

Tears filled his eyes as he began to break down, "God is telling...he's telling me something and I'm listening!"

Sammy let go of me and backed away from my bedside. This is starting to get freaky. I hope he doesn't do anything crazy. I don't have the energy to fight with him tonight. He's pacing the floor and speaking in broken up sentences like he's thinking of what to do to me. The least he can do is take his hands out of his pockets.

"What's going on? Tell me right now," I demanded.

"I can't keep treating you the way I do!" He finally shouted, "God's not going to allow it anymore."

Sammy blatantly pointed at me in the dark. The longer he stood there the creepier I felt looking back at him. I'm so tired and I have no idea what to do I'm just listening to his rant, terrified. I mean, I did chase him with a knife today.

"Sammy, you're not making any sense...you're scaring me."

"When you die, I die…I can't live my life this way… or without you."

"Come to bed you've been drinking, baby, come lay down."

I threw the sheets back to lure him into bed, while trying to blow off everything he said until the morning comes. That way he can make a little more sense to me.

"When you got shot you should've been dead," he said, capturing my attention.

"Not tonight, Sammy, please lay down," I begged.

"That year, when you first met me," he reminisced, "Remember you said you'd always regret that year… you should've been dead, Stacy."

His low, shaky voice was stone cold. The horrible memory made my hair stand on end. Sammy once again began to pace the floor in a disturbed state, heavily panting and significantly sweating. Now I was completely wrapped up in his rant. Where's this coming from? Why is he talking like this? My heart began to pound in my throat.

"I'm killing you more every day," he said throwing both his arms up high in an appalling gesture.

I am completely baffled, 'Why would he say that? What happened to him today? I have never seen him this way.'

"I was with some of the fellas downtown."

Sammy paused for a moment to take in a deep breath. Before he could finish he began to break down sobbing again. Sammy dropped to the floor and buried his face in his palms. I jumped out of bed and crouched down on the floor beside him. kissing his forehead repeatedly, I held him in my arms.

"I felt, I felt something…and I thought of you," he paused, "I saw you! Like you were there with me and it made me want to come home to you and my kids!"

I don't know what to expect I'm not following his story or what he was going to tell me next. I just want him to get in the bed and go to sleep, damn it! I thought I knew where he was going with this, but all I can do is sit here and listen in amazement.

"So, I…I got in the car on my way home and Terrell paged me, I stopped and called Grandma Vicky's… somebody killed two of the guys I was with."

Whoa. When I heard that I held onto him tighter. I thought back to the time Janessa tried to run him over. This is different. This is someone else that doesn't love him.

"I was there, Stacy…shouldn't I be dead, too?"

Everything in me was numb. In this moment, God is letting me know that he was listening to me. He's been listening all along, and he's got a plan. I helped Sammy up from the floor, got him out of his sweaty clothes and into bed. As we lay there, him asleep in my arms, I began process everything Sammy was saying.

The year I met Sammy, was one I will never forget so long as I live. Me, Janessa, Sammy, and Terrell went to a party in South Aurora. There were so many people there dancing in the dark and acting weird, like they were in slow motion. The place was filled with smoke and ridiculously loud music. Over and over I begged Sammy to take me home, but he wanted to stay and party. The last thing I truly remember was Janessa rubbing up on Sammy in the living room against the wall. They slow danced a couple times before Terrell asked me to dance. Of course, I said no he was supposed to be with Janessa. What I believe happened was Sammy got so tired of my complaining and he told someone to make me a drink, just to shut me up. There was something in it. I remember feeling dizzy and anxious. My heart throbbed and beat excessively inside of my chest. Next thing I knew a guy, who I thought was Sammy, pulled me into a quiet place. It grew very dark and very scary fast. I was so doped up I thought it was a dream or a nightmare that I was having. I was so out of touch.

Though in reality, I was being taken advantage of by four different people including a girl. I was carried out of the party and thrown into a pool. Witnesses on my case said they watched a group of people throw someone from the balcony into a pool two stories below. Everyone was doped up and partied out, they thought it was all a part of the party, just kids having fun. About an hour later, I was stumbled upon by three drunken idiots who were most likely at the party, too. I stayed in the hospital for six weeks to rid my body of three different kinds of diseases that were thankfully all able to be treated. My left arm was broken from the plunge and I had been bleeding internally. Then, I was only fourteen years old going on fifteen just the week after the party. Sammy's right, I should've been dead. Why am I not? Surely, I have been placed here on earth for a reason just like everyone else. Out of the blue, Sammy sat up.

"Stacy, tomorrow we have to do something to get these demons out of our lives…we've been given a second chance…I want to do it right."

I began to smile, for the first time in a long time, I smiled at Sammy. We slept so peacefully that night, our bodies were intertwined with one another holding on tighter than the Earth and the moon. Never really wanting to let go if time will hold us together, we will be forever.

"Stacy, baby wake up," Sammy softly called out to me.

I woke up to each of my babies smacking my face and patting my chest to get me up. He placed a big plate of hot food in my lap and kissed my forehead.

"Telephone."

"Who is it?" I questioned, curious to know who gets up this early.

Sammy smiled at me as he sat at the foot of the bed twisting the knob of the television set. Sigh. I slowly lifted the phone to my ear.

"Hello," I answered reluctantly.

"What's up, cousin," Dominic said excited.

Instantly, I began to sob. I sat my plate aside and made sure my babies were secure in the middle of the bed. Then wrapped my arms around Sammy's neck. He took the phone and placed it back in my hand.

"Talk to your cousin, baby," he urged, "he missed you."

# Epiphany

There's been a change in both Sammy and I the kids know their daddy better than they used to. I'm so happy my cousin Dominic no longer has hatred or anger for Sammy like he used to. I guess they talked it out I wasn't going to ask how or why? I'm just glad that they did. Sammy really manned up, he doesn't want to be reminded of who he used to be. Every Sunday morning, the four of us are in church and afterwards Sammy takes us out for lunch. Now, I don't work because Sammy doesn't want me to. He says that I deserve to be a stay at home mom and keeps me looking good week by week. Though, if I choose to then I can work. On days that he isn't working, we take the kids out to the park or somewhere nice for family time! Time that we never thought we had we now spend together happily. No more beatings, no more arguing, fighting or fussing. We also added a new member to our family! Another boy we named Martin Jacobs.

I'm a nineteen-year old mother of three and this is my crazy life. I have sixty years or more ahead of me. Years that I want to spend raising my children and my grandchildren with my lifelong love.

# Love and Life

It's the new millennium! Corey and Chane are now both seventeen and growing older every passing day. My little man, Martin, was sixteen looking more and more like his daddy every day. We moved up in life and found a beautiful three-bedroom two-bathroom house, Sam insisted. Our boys went to school a short bus ride away and were always into something. Every week I got a call about them ditching school, smoking on school grounds, fighting or something else I felt to be backwards and unnecessary. Though, there is very little that I can do to keep them on the straight and narrow. Sam doesn't approve of their behavior either, but now that their older they're completely immune to ass whippings. They do the same things Sam used to when we were younger, and I feel some things are far worse than others, especially when my boys beat on each other.

Overall, we're honest with the boys, so they are honest with us. We don't hide anything, and we've allowed them to be free to do whatever we deem is okay or not. The boys obey my house rules as well as their fathers'. I just have to keep reminding them to obey the rules away from home, too.

## Summer Break 2006

At the beginning of my boys' summer break I worried if their last day of school was a good one. As usual, I was the first to return home after a long day of work. I cleaned up and cooked for Sam and the kids. Afterwards, I sat in the TV room and waited for all my boys to return home. A couple hours into my peaceful time alone, Martin stormed into the house with a bruised and bleeding face. I could tell he was very upset because my baby boy was punching at the walls as he angrily approached the bathroom down the hall.

"Martin!" I yelled franticly rushing behind him to the sink to clean him up, "What happened to your face?"

"I'm good, Mom, you should see the other kid...

these fools tried to jump me I was just defending myself," he confessed, breathing heavy.

"Okay, don't worry about it sweet heart, where are your brothers?"

The twins rushed inside cheering for their baby brother joined by two of their close friends, "Martin! Martin! Martin!" they went on pumping their fists in the air.

"Corey, Chane what happened to my baby?" I asked of them, impatiently waiting for an answer, "Everett, Reggie what happened?"

"He's fine momma, some fool was trying to jump on him, so he did what he was supposed to do and fought back," Corey replied with a smile.

"Yeah, momma he's a rider," Chane added.

I scoffed at Chane's comment and continued to dab Martin's wounds.

"So, I'm down?" Martin questioned with open arms and his face in my grip.

"Yeah little man you down," Reggie said to Martin, "You with it."

"Baby, I'm home," the sound of relief, Sam peered around the corner of the bathroom doorway, shocked by what he seen, "Boy, what done happened to your face?"

"You know your kids', they up there at that school fighting again," I replied patting the open soar on Martin's busted lip.

"But he stuck in there, pops." Everett told him, "He didn't get beat up or nothing."

"Okay, clean yourself up, son, I want you all in the family room," Sam demanded, "I got surprises for all of my boys!"

Martin jumped up abruptly and brushed past me. We all gathered in the front room awaiting the supposed good news that Sam had. On the floor there were about six boxes wrapped in pretty paper; some big, some wide, some long and some small.

"Just pick one and open it...don't matter which one, these are for all my boys."

Each of the boys opened one gift. After they had all been unwrapped they put the pieces of equipment together. They had their own recording studio setup: a microphone, a keyboard, speakers, notebooks, headphones, pens and lots of wires and blank CD's.

"Now take this downstairs and make me a hit," Sam said with a chuckle.

The boys each grabbed something and took it into the basement to set it all up. No later than about three hours we began to hear music and our lyrical princes showing off their skills. I was shocked by the expensive gifts, but I didn't ask any questions. Sam felt the tension.

"Don't worry," Sam assured me.

The boys have been in and out of the house with a new friend each time ever since Sam got their studio equipment. I still wonder how he was able to pay for all that stuff. Sam and I sat in the kitchen at the table enjoying breakfast alone.

"Listen to them go," I started.

"Yeah," Sam agreed, his face buried in today's paper, "Makes me so proud."

"I'm still in the dark about where you got that stuff, Sam."

"Oh, Stace," he began with a deep exhale, folding

the paper in half, "Don't you worry yourself with that."

I trusted him, now that we were happy with our lives, deep in my heart I believed in him. Our mortgage is covered and Sam's paying off both vehicles. The boys, well, I believe Corey works. But they buy their own stuff. Sam collected his plate and placed it in the sink.

"Sure," I responded, "I trust you; you know that?"

"I know, baby," He said headed out of the kitchen, then doubled back, "Do you need anything before I go?"

"No."

I decided to stay home from work today. I had a strange feeling about leaving the boys alone. I want to keep an eye on things around the house. About a dozen of their friends are in the basement bumping and jumping to their new songs. It didn't bother me to listen to my boys' creative music day by day, however, by the evening which was around nine or ten o'clock for them, they knew to turn the volume down. I fell fast asleep around one o'clock that afternoon. My boys left me asleep as they snuck a few girls down into the basement.


**(Knock...Knock, knock)**


I was awakened by an uncertain knock at the door. I got up out of my comfortable space on the couch and lazily walked over to get it, "who is it?"

No answer. I asked once again.

"Whose there," but still no answer.

When I peeked out the window I couldn't see far enough. *Sigh* I began to remove the chain and unlock the door, the music was so loud they couldn't hear me. When I opened it, there was a young man standing on the other side of my screen in red sagging shorts and no shirt. He had a strong physique, his skin red, brown and he was riddled with tattoos. The young boy had long, jet black braids and hazel eyes like my mother. Parked along the street was a red Suburban truck with music blaring. There were at least seven or eight guys standing around each side locked, loaded and ready to fight.

"Hey Miss Lady, I'm looking for Martin, is he here?" The boy asked politely.

Every now and then he would glance back at the group behind him. I felt my entire body weakening on me as I caught on to what was happening. My legs felt like they were glued to the floor.

"Hold on let me see, what's your name, sweetie?" I asked the boy that frightened me so, yet he smiled back.

"Just let him know Rodney is here to see him."

Slowly, I headed down into the basement. Rodney's deep, demanding voice rang in my mind like a gong. When the boys heard my footsteps, they cut down the music and every pair of eyes in the room stuck onto me.

"Martin," I began, "A boy named Rodney, is here to see you."

Martin, seated next to a beautiful girl, gave me his full attention. Corey tossed down his pen and paper then rushed over to me.

"Momma, what did he say to you?" Corey questioned

Fear gripped my heart and I began to sulk.

"Don't let him hurt my baby," I begged, glaring up at Corey, "Do something, Chane don't let them hurt my baby."

"Nah," Chane responded dashing up the stairs.

At least ten other kids rushed up the stairs and out the front door. I went into the kitchen grabbed my pack of cigarettes as well as the phone. Just in case I had to call Sam's cellular to get him home. Then, cautiously made my way out the front door onto the porch.

"You already got smashed at school now you want to come and get smashed at my crib," Martin said taunting him, "How you find my house, bro?"

"You snuck me blood, but it's good," Rodney replied squaring up with Martin toe to toe.

My legs were too weak to stand. I crouched down on the steps and watched in horror. Martin stood in the middle of the street squared up neck and neck with Rodney. Once they began to fight I was already finished with one entire cigarette. Rodney rushed Martin and landed a few good hits on his face. Though, Martin came back with a hard hitter to the face and neck. Causing Rodney to fall to the ground. Martin kicked him in his face, his stomach and stomped on him a couple times until the blood from his mouth began to spew.

"My sons a murderer," I joked as I lit another cigarette, tears crowding my eyes.

Rodney sprung up off the ground, picked up my

baby and body slammed him, "Ah! Martin, my baby, my baby, no, no, no! Corey! Chane!"

The cigarette flung out of my hands. Everything in me wanted to grab my son.

"Momma, calm down, let him fight!" Chane yelled, as both my twins held me back.

The group in the Suburban truck seemed completely unaffected. They stood by and watched with smiles on their faces. Rodney leaned over Martin landing punches at his face and torso. Suddenly, the fighting ceased as Martin rose to his feet and Rodney took in a few deep breaths. Each of the boys began to spit in the street, coughing up blood. They squared up once again, ready to turn this minor fight into a full fledge war between the two. Rodney's people stood watch waiting for their warrior to prevail, as did we.

"Get him Martin!" the girls cheered my son on.

Martin ducked and dodged at Rodney's hits. He landed a couple more punches to the face then finally knocked Rodney off his feet again. I began to worry even more. There are at least three out of five of those guys over twenty-one years old. At least. I'm praying the other guys wouldn't try to do anything to my kids.

"Yeah, that's what I'm talking about! That's my little bro!" Chane screamed in exhilaration.

"Like I said you're not seeing me," Martin said to Rodney before waltzing away.

Everyone paraded back into my house. Meanwhile I watched as one of Rodney's much older companions got out of the driver seat of the red truck and headed over to him. The rest of the people followed behind, I assume, to help Rodney. Still, on the ground in the middle of the street he was bruised and battered. Only to be beaten once again by the entire crew of five to six men. The men piled back into the truck, leaving Rodney bleeding and badly hurt. Luckily, they didn't run over him as they drove past. Reluctant, I rose from the porch frozen in my place. I could hear Rodney coughing and grunting as I inched my way over to aid him. Martin spied out the window from the front room, then brought out a wet towel and some bandage wraps. Martin helped me take Rodney into the backyard where the twins wouldn't see us helping. We propped Rodney up in a lawn chair on our gazebo like patio. I figured with the summer coming up he won't be cold during the night. I can't allow him to come inside until I know for sure that he's going to be welcomed.

"Why is you helping me, blood?" Rodney questioned; his left eye nearly shut.

"Unlike my brothers I sympathize for people like you."

I'm proud of my son, "Are you hungry, Rodney?"

He studied the ground for answers and kept his head hung low. Rodney used his shorts to wipe blood from his face.

"Yes, ma'am…please."

"Martin, your father is going to be home soon," I started, "We're going to have to explain this to him."

Martin glared at me with a worried look in his brown eyes as he nodded his head in agreement. My baby patted Rodney on the shoulder before guiding me inside. I made a huge pot of spaghetti for my boys and their uninvited guests. That kept everyone in the basement distracted, so Martin can help me with

Rodney. We brought Rodney a full plate and a glass of ice-cold water. Martin and I sat in shock as we watched Rodney devour the plate.

"Hey man, slow down," Martin teased, "You act like you haven't eaten in years."

"You see me every day at school," Rodney began, his mouth full of food, "The clothes I wear."

"Them fools you be with," Martin cut in.

Rodney took a second to swallow before responding.

"Omar is my family...now, I don't have them either."

"Where is your mother? Is Omar your brother?" I asked, curious to know.

"Adopted," Rodney blankly expressed, "Omar took me in from the foster home we grew up in together; he always looked out for me."

The thought hasn't crossed my mind for quite some time, but I wonder how my baby boy is doing. Now, he would be about nineteen years old. Just a year older than my twins and two years over my baby boy. My eyes locked onto Martin's.

"I'll be right back," My baby boy said, before leaping out of sight.

Martin went inside and came back with fresh clothes and blankets, "You can stay here, then," he offered.

Martin returned inside before peeking at my neutral reaction. There are no objections from me, especially if this young man has nowhere left to go. My only concern would be how Sam and the twins would react.

"Well, if my baby said it that's what it's going to

be," I told him, "We don't know who you are, son, just be good to us."

"Yes ma'am."

"We'll be good to you," I continued, "Give me that plate."

Rodney handed over the empty platter. Just before I turned to walk away I felt a strong grip on my wrist. I doubled back and looked down upon Rodney's battered face. He peered up at me with the most beautiful hazel eyes. The eye that was opened anyway.

"What's your name?" Rodney asked gazing into my face.

"You call me, Ms. Stacy."

"Stacy, that's a beautiful name," he complimented.

Slowly Rodney released his grip on my wrist. I snapped out of the trance and came back to reality, took the covers and placed them over Rodney.

"You better get some rest, in the morning we'll talk about your place in this house," I suggested with a worried smile upon my face.

"Thank you, Ms. Stacy."

I walked over to shut the door of our sheltered patio then returned inside. All I could think is what if it's him? The baby boy we tried to forget and leave in the past. I walked into the kitchen and placed the dirty plate in the dish water then leaned against the counter. I heard the knob jiggling as the lock turned and Sam crossed the threshold of the front door.

"Wife!" Sam joked before joining me in the kitchen.

He caressed me and kissed my face over and over. Sam leaned back and peered into my eyes. He could tell that there was something very wrong.

"Is everything okay, baby," he questioned, "The boys are okay?"

I hesitated and let out a deep sigh, "We need to have a family talk."

Before I could say another word, Sam stormed out the kitchen and to the top of the basement stairs, "Boys! Get the hell up here now!"

My legs reached Sam before my words. Before an even bigger misunderstanding occurred.

"No, Sam it's not the twins," I said rushing over to him, "Martin and I have something to tell you...to tell you all."

"What's up, pop," Corey began.

The twins reached the top of the stairs, confused. They were automatically in defense mode.

"The police did not come," Chane confessed.

"Boys, Sam come in the kitchen," I urged.

Curious, the three of them followed close behind. Along the way, I was making up what I was going to say in my mind. Hopefully the words come out right.

"What's going on, Mom?" Chane asked first.

"Where's Martin?" Corey chimed in.

The four of us gathered around the table and took a seat. I didn't know how to begin without my boys flying off on Martin. Or, Sam flying off on me. Honestly, if I wore a tie I'd be loosening it up. And, dabbing the beads of sweat on my forehead with a snot rag.

"Nobody get loose, okay," I began, "I helped the boy..."

"You helped Rodney?" Chane interrupted.

"Why did you do that?" Corey shouted, "They would've shot our house up!"

Sam rested his chin on his fist, "What happened today? Tell me right now, Stacy!"

"These fools came to the door to get Martin this time," Chane began, "They would've tried to jump him again if we weren't with him."

"Omar, he wants all of our heads," Corey added, "Everett's and Reggie's, too."

"I know you boys keep dog food," Sam expressed, "That's not the point of all this...what's the point, Stace?"

"I told Martin that it was okay to let the boy stay here," I spat, waiting for the fists to fly.

"Stay where?" Sam started to get angry, "Answer me!"

My lips didn't part. Sam screamed as he slapped his palm down on our glass table. Chane and Corey began to grow equally as angry as their father. Sam stood to his feet, placed his hands in his pockets and paced the floor. The twins sat silent with the same blank expression looking to me for answers

"Mom," Corey started.

"I'm going to ask one more time," Sam continued, "Who's in my house?"

Before I had the chance to respond, Martin walked inside from the backyard where Rodney was propped up in a chair. Bruised and battered. Martin walked into the tense situation with an empty glass in hand and a confident look in his eyes.

"You already told them, Mom?" Martin asked, "You should've let me do it."

He crossed the kitchen, placed the glass in the sink water with the other dishes then turned to face his father. My poor child was frozen right where he stood with Sam impatiently waiting on an explanation. Sam's bulky arms crossed over his chest.

"I'm listening," he said, leaning in toward Martin.

"Pop," He began with a huge exhale, "I believe that there is a reason for everything."

"Are you stupid?" Corey hollered as he jumped out of his seat.

Corey leaped across the kitchen and lunged at Martin. Luckily, Sam stood between them before any punches were thrown.

"Stop it!" I shouted, "Sit down Corey!"

Though, the fighting insisted. Nothing died down in the house until about eleven o'clock. Martin and I attempted to explain to his brothers and father that Rodney is welcome to stay with us. Finally, Sam had come to his senses.

"I don't care what you guys say he can stay here, Mom, already said it was okay."

"Are you serious?" Chane exclaimed.

"Your stupid man, you must've lost it," Corey agreed, "Maybe he hit you in the head too hard, bro."

"Yeah, he did," Chane joined in.

"I don't have a problem with it," I added, "besides, I've always taught you boys to give more than you take, so you will be blessed in the end...right?"

I have never been so proud of, Martin, "He doesn't have nowhere else to go...Omar, don't want him around."

"Omar is going to use him to get to us," Corey yelled, "Am I the only one that peeps that."

"Corey's right," Chane chimed in, "Martin, this ain't smart bro."

Sam massaged his face, "What about the boy's family?"

"He's a foster kid," Martin added.

Sam locked eyes with me from across the kitchen. Now, he knows what I'm feeling. I stood by the counter with my arms folded over my chest, glaring at Sam and his many reactions. I watched his face relax as he slipped into deep thought.

"Who is Omar?" Sam questioned.

"He's nobody," Corey angrily responded.

"Okay," Sam raised his eyebrows, "Where's this other kid at?"

Awe stricken I stood silent for a moment. I love my husband he changes more and more as the years go by. We tell the boys everything. Although, I never knew how to tell them that they have an older brother. Not only that, I don't know where he is.

"On the patio," I responded, "I fed him and gave him a blanket."

Sam walked over to the sliding doors and peered out at Rodney dozing off in the lawn chair. Me, Martin and the twins stayed in the kitchen. Our eyes glanced around the room at one another anticipating on Sam's response.

"He can stay," Sam announced as he entered the kitchen.

"What!" The twins spoke out in unison.

Sam glided across the room toward his place at the table. He stood over the boys and tilted his head down as he scanned their faces. The twins were angry and confused while Martin sat silent, emotionless.

"How do you boys know this kid?" He finally questioned.

"School," Corey spat.

"He runs with Omar and a few guys that we don't deal with," Chane explained messaging his face.

From across the room, I turned my back and pretended to clean. Chane is right. I just watched this kid fight my son, but Martin wants him here. Honestly, there seems to be a little more going on than what the boys are telling us.

Martin cleared his throat, "Rodney lives with Omar now, but he used to just run around school campus and be in our classes...we used to be cool with him."

"Used to be," Corey added, still angry.

I stopped leaned against the countertop and faced the table, folding my arms tightly over my chest.

"Corey," Sam started as he took his seat at the table, "Say your peace, son."

"What if we can't trust him?" Corey began, looking to Martin, "Then, what?"

They each glared at one another with the same blank expression as I stood watch from the counter. My arms still nervously folded over my chest.

Martin spoke with confidence, "Why can't we? We called him brother, so I trust him."

Corey didn't say another word, he slowly left the table and made his way back into the basement. Chane followed. Martin and Sam remained seated in silence as Sam licked his fingertips, flipping through todays paper. Just as I turned my back to once again pretend I wasn't in the room, Chane and Corey returned with their "smoke box."

"Martin," Corey shouted from the hall.

"Yo."

"Come on," Chane chimed in.

Martin scattered out of the kitchen and outside with the twins. With a huge grin, I peeked over my shoulder at Sam. My love was glued to the paper. Although, neither of my twin boys agreed with us they each went out into the backyard space where Rodney was surely over hearing our conversation. My boys gathered around him and began a smoke session in celebration of a brother.

"Welcome to the family, Rod," Martin broke the awkward silence, "Pops said you can stay, too."

"More like welcome back," Chane added.

Rodney sighed in disbelief. There was still tension from the twins even though they were clearly trying to push past it.

"Thanks man, I don't know how to repay your mom, but I'll get a job or something and help around the house, whatever, just say the word."

"You already know how we get down," Chane told him as they shook hands.

"You remember...brother," Corey added, "We look out for each other."

Rodney looked to Corey in disbelief, then turned his eye to Chane. Finally, he peered at Martin tears streaming as he bowed his head. Rodney was timid, afraid and a little reluctant to speak.

"No hard feelings?" Martin asked, holding out his hand for a response.

He gleefully picked his head up and looked to Martin once again. A tear slipped down Rodney's cheek as a smile stretched across his worried face.

"No hard feelings," Rodney shook his hand in agreement.

Chane continued to loom over him, "Let's leave the past in the past."

"But, when Omar finds out," Corey added, "We got to be ready...that means you, too, Rod."

Rodney sat himself up comfortably. Nodding his head in agreement.

"I could care less about what happens to them," Rodney confessed, "Look at what they did to me."

"I'm going to call Reggie and let him know what's up," Chane said just before disappearing into the house.

Rodney wanted to set the record straight, he felt that something needed to be said. Something that reveals exactly where he stands from this day going forward.

"I'm still a brother?" He began with tears crowding his eyes.

Corey took a long pull of the blunt as he peered across to Martin, then back to Rodney and passed him the blunt, "You look like us...blood isn't everything."

Chane rushed back out onto the patio with good news, "Everett and Reggie know now...pass the blunt bro," he said tapping Rodney.

Rodney smiled as another tear crept down his brown, soggy cheek. Sam and I watched from the other side of the glass, listening in close.

"Do you think it's going to work?" Sam asked with doubt.

"I do."

# Sanctuary

Rodney has done exactly what he promised that sad day. He's gotten better and only by God's good graces he was able to get a job. Rodney showed us the loyalty. He brought even more to the table. Side hustles out the backyard of the house with the boys brought a little extra money to the table every month. I have no idea that it's happening, of course. For the most part, the boys got along just fine more than Sam and I could have imagined. Martin shares his room with Rodney. To make him feel a little more at home, we had gone and bought him a mattress, a dresser, and even some new clothes. Rodney and Martin were becoming close, like the twins. The two-year gap in age wasn't an issue because Rodney was small for nineteen going on twenty. Every morning, Sam and I would go to work and return home to a clean house, nice music and the smell of Pine-Sol. Thanks to the extra help.

The ultimate women's movie was on in the family room where I seated myself with a glass of wine. This feels more than deserved, especially because my boys usually get to my bottles before me. I can't wait until everyone else comes home. Rodney and I were the only two here for the first time. Sam had gone to work, and the twins took Martin to his court appearance for fighting, again. They decided to wait around downtown until he was finished with his two hours of community service. They think that me and their father were born yesterday. I know what they're down there doing. I just wonder why Rodney stayed behind? Probably to make sure no money fell through the cracks. I complain and talk until I'm blue in the face, but Sam doesn't say anything. I know for a fact if anything were to happen to one of my babies, he would be the first one to jump bad. Though, I would have to jump badder than that.

Rodney came out the backroom and into the family room interrupting my crazy, random thoughts.

"Ms. Stacy," he nervously called out to me, "Is it okay if I sit here with you and watch the movie?"

A smile stretched across my face as I happily welcomed him.

"Sure, honey, sit down."

My arms flung open, gesturing for Rodney to seat himself on the couch right next to me.

"Come on, son, sit here."

Rodney gleefully scurried around the couch and plopped down.

"What is this?"

"It's about this woman who did bad things, and she would throw her baby in the trash. One day, someone found the baby, the baby was adopted. The real mother fought to get him back."

"My mama gave me up, too," Rodney said, shrugging his shoulders, "Can I have some wine?"

"That's fine, son."

I smiled and threw my arm around him, downing the bitter drink from the bottle. We sat through half of the movie, the other half I was distracted by Rodney's fidgeting and sudden movements. Maybe I shouldn't have gave him any of my wine.

"Let me ask you something, Rodney?"

"What's up, Mom," he responded quickly.

It was almost as if he was waiting for me to ask him. I stopped short and glared into his familiar face. Rodney's hazel eyes and his red-brown skin compelled me.

"Where did you come from?"

"I don't know."

His expression was blank. I studied his tone then questioned his response.

"What do you mean, son?"

"I always been in foster care," he told me, "I know I was born at Denver Health."

"D G," I said with a smile.

"Yeah,"

Rodney giggled. Before he continued, I picked up the channel changer and turned the volume on the television down.

"So, you were born in Denver?" I asked.

"Yeah," he began, then took another sip from the bottle, "My mama was like sixteen when she had me."

"Oh my God."

My heart jumped into my throat as I tried to contain myself. Goosebumps rolled down my spine as chills spread throughout my body. I began to flare with emotion. Tears crowded my eyes, my fingers started to lock up and went numb.

"It's okay, Mom," he said with a smile, "I'm good."

Through his confident smile, I could see the hurt and confusion on his face. I rose to my feet and slapped my hands against my face. Whimpers came from deep within me as I attempted to hold back. I took in a deep breath, then tried to ask him more questions.

"And you're nineteen, right?"

He slowly rose to his feet, cautiously turned his back to me and took a few short cautious steps away with his hands up.

"I just turned nineteen," he responded.

"Oh my God!"

"What?" He shouted, backing further away from me.

We stood in the middle of the family room floor, my eyes locked onto his. Finally, my hands left my face and reached out to Rodney. He carefully came to me and grabbed a hold of each of my hands.

"What is it, Mom?" Rodney said softly.

I brushed my hands over his face, then cupped his head in my palms. For a moment, I was completely lost in his eyes. I see myself, I see Sam, I see my mother and if I only knew him. I'd probably see my father in Rodney, too. Breaking down, I confessed.

"I gave my baby boy away."

The strong grip Rodney had on my palms began to loosen up.

"How could you do that?" He questioned.

"I was afraid for his life," I cried, "Sam, was trying to kill us."

"What?" Rodney shouted again, "So, you give up your baby."

He tossed my hands from his grip and retreated to the other side of the room. Rodney put his hands on his sides and hung his head low as he paced the floor. I sprinted across the room after him and spun Rodney around so that he could look into my eyes.

"Sam wouldn't go away," I started, "No matter where I went or how much I begged he just wouldn't leave me alone. So, I gave my baby away to save him."

"How safe do you think he was with the state?" Rodney boldly questioned.

My head filled with pressure and my eyes grew wide as I fell to Rodney's feet. He dropped to the floor with me, wrapped me in his arms and rested his chin on top of my head.

"I'm sorry I just love you," he expressed, rubbing my back, "You're not her."

"Oh my God!" I shouted in tears, "I'm so confused."

"I'm confused, too, Mom."

We both laughed. We laughed so hard that love filled the room. In the midst, I felt multiple drops fall on my shoulder. Rodney's tears rolled down the back of my right arm. It made me cry again. This time, we cried tears of joy.

"The boys know?" I questioned, snatching myself away, "You all already know this?"

Rodney cut in, "No, no we just called each other

brothers because we looked alike and I was always with them making mone-"

He stopped short. Not realizing I already know. I see the bags for the dog food I just don't see the dogs.

"It's okay, son, this is just between us, okay?"

I took a deep breath and once again, wrapped him tight in my arms.

He nodded in agreement with me, "Yes ma'am, just the two of us.

I could not sleep at all I felt horrible. There's this little voice in the back of my head telling me this might be a mistake. Obviously, Rodney is not my son. It would be the biggest coincidence of the century. I lay wide awake watching repeats of Beatrice Arthur until around four o'clock in the morning, before getting up to turn off the set. Climbing back into bed with Sam I cuddled up underneath him on my way to sweet dreams. Suddenly, I heard a thud coming from the other side of my bedroom door. Once again, I quietly slid out of the sheets and inched my way over to open it. In the darkness I heard the door to Martin and Rodney's room down the hall shut. I took a breath glared down at the ground and there it was. An envelope, with my name incorrectly spelled on it. Though, what the letter says is tickling me more than anything. I picked it up quietly closed the door and locked it behind me. Sam tossed and turned in the bed as I slowly sat on top of the blankets. I smiled laughing to myself in the darkness. I leaned over into the light next to the bed and read in my mind:

*In the dark depths of the night when*
*you my love can't sleep,*
*Close your eyes and wipe the tears no*
*longer do you have to weep.*
*When you feel alone with no one to hold*
*and only the memories of he,*
*Remember you can count on a soul, a soul such as me.*
*With your eyes so brown and your heart full of love,*
*I was truly sent a blessing that came from above.*
*You smile upon me with oceans of happiness,*
*Seeing you alive more makes me feel dead less.*
*To the love I know as Stacy, I hope one day you can see,*
*That your heart is truly safe in the hands of me*

*Love,*
*Rodney*

Over excitement bloated in my heart. I had developed new feelings for someone that loved me more than I could understand. At the same damn time I felt terribly guilty. Like I was hiding something from Sam. I left the bathroom and hid the letter in the bottom drawer next to my bed.

"I love you, baby," I said gazing over at Sam.

Rodney had been standing on the other side of my door listening closely. He heard me; the pitter pat of sneaking feet scurried in the hallway. Rodney once again returned to the room that he shared with Martin and lay in his bed comfortably. He threw his arms behind his head and glared at the ceiling.

"Thank the Lord for you, Stacy," he prayed as he let out a deep sigh and smiled.

No matter how hard I tried, I couldn't stop my thoughts. I couldn't get to sleep. I had the undeniable urge to get out of bed and try to get Rodney up, too. Once again, I crept out of bed and down the hall on the tip of my toes.

"Rodney, sweetie, are you still awake?" I whispered.

I quietly wrapped on the door, then entered the room with a million thoughts going through my mind at once. Through the darkness I could see Rodney cautiously raise up from his pillows. With my arm I gestured for him to come out of the room. Rodney rose up completely and tip-toed behind me down the hall to the back patio.

"Rodney, son, what's going on with you?"

He kept his eyes down the entire time avoiding contact and fidgeting with his hands.

"I'm sorry, Mom I just wanted to tell you how I feel."

"No, I'm talking about that guy," I started, "Omar?"

Rodney jerked his neck back in amazement, just like Sam used to do to me. A slight smile stretched over his face then he began to frown. I know he thought I brought him out here for something else. I can't help what he thinks. I need to know what I need to know.

"...Omar was my big homey and he thinks I turned my back on him to be here."

"Was he one of the guys that came with you that day?" I questioned, "You turned your back on the same people that turned their backs on you."

Rodney sat in shame with nothing to say. He

messaged the back of his neck then rested his chin on his fist. I could tell that he had something that he needed to say, but he just didn't know how to say it.

"You don't understand," he responded, "I'm bringing all my money to you and the house…he still wants me to bring him the money."

"Okay," I said puzzled, "Have you been over there recently?"

Rodney bowed his head again shamefully. I was afraid that he might have gone back to those people. No matter how good we tried to be to him. Those people are familiar to Rodney.

"Son," I said placing my hand on his, "I want you to be honest with me, I'm only trying to help make your situation better."

"They saw me down the street walking with, Martin," he expressed, "So, I went to Omar."

"What did he say to you?" I asked.

"I tried to convince him that I was just coming here to get some food and shower, I told him that I don't live here," Rodney confessed, "He told me to bring him the money and the dog food and they won't come back here."

"Oh no," I said placing both hands over my heart.

"Omar already had problems with the twins," he continued, cautious with his words, "The clucks go back and forth between us knowing that they shouldn't."

"So, that's why he came?" I asked, "The boys are taking the money out of his pocket."

Rodney buried his face in his sweaty palms and took a deep breath, "If anything happens it's my fault."

The news shocked me, though I gave him a hug. Rodney bowed his head shamefully. Wrapping his arms around my neck tight.

"I'm sorry, Ms. Stacy," he pleaded.

"I know, son," I told him as I held onto him tight, "They're not going to hurt you."

I leaned back to look him in the eyes, though Rodney's eyes were glued to the ground.

"Rodney, baby, thank you for being honest with me," his eyes blood red, swollen from crying, "We have to let the boys know and Sam, too."

"Okay, I'm just scared," he told me, "I don't want to die, I don't want no one to die."

I squeezed him tighter, "No one is going to die, okay."

I could feel him nodding in agreement, though his face still buried in shame. Rodney was so afraid that I began to get scared myself. We stood there for a moment before I felt the need to break the silence.

"I didn't mean to upset you," I expressed, "Let's go back to bed?"

He finally glared into my eyes, "Ms. Stacy…I want you to be a part of my life and I don't want to screw yours up…or theirs."

I smiled, "I love you, honey, and I am a part of your life…I'm here for you, do you understand me?"

"Yes, ma'am."

"Just be there for us when we need you."

I calmed him down, "Come on, Sam's alarm is going to go off any minute now and I'd best be in the bed when it does."

# A New Day

The next morning started off with a big breakfast before the day began for us. One by one, each of the boys retrieved to the kitchen and chose a spot at the table.

"Good morning, Momma," Corey greeted me, as he took the first seat.

"It smells good in here," Chane was the next to greet me "morning, Mom."

He kissed my cheek and went to the cupboard for a glass. Chane filled his cup with orange juice, then took his place at the table as well.

"Good morning, good morning to you and you, good morning wife…good morning sunny day," Sam praised the new day with glory, "God is good."

Martin and Rodney came out into the kitchen in unison, yawning as they stretched their arms.

"Good morning, yo."

Martin said aloud with a smile. Rodney shyly walked in behind.

"Good morning, boys," Sam responded, sipping his coffee with his nose stuck in the paper.

From over my left shoulder I stole a glance at Rodney and smiled. He shyly smiled back and conspicuously kept his head low. Martin noticed the exchange of gestures between us and grew angry with suspicion.

"I think everyone should be very satisfied with this meal," I complimented on my skilled cooking.

"What's up with the big breakfast, Mom?" Corey questioned.

"Yeah," Chane added, "What's the occasion?"

"I'm just in a good mood baby," I smiled, "That's all."

I brought each container and platter of food to the table carefully. Martin was hung up on the sudden happiness in both me and Rodney.

"Hurry up and eat, bro," Chane urged Corey, "We got that thing, you know."

"Yup," Corey responded scarfing down his meal.

"What "thing"?" I questioned.

The twins remained silent. Corey and Chane continued reaching and grabbing food. As if I never said a word.

"I'm sure they're fine, baby," Sam spoke from behind the paper.

After breakfast, I went out onto the front porch and had my annual cigarette as I watched the morning form. Chane and Corey were out the door without saying goodbye. Sam is right, those two will be just fine. Martin came out to join me on the porch.

"Mom, what's going on?"

He glared into my face and instantly noticed the guilt. A wave of anxiety rushed me as the overwhelming feeling of shame blanketed me.

"Rodney loves you, Momma," Martin enlightened me.

"I have a big heart, just like you...*sigh* he looks just like you boys," I confessed.

Martin jerked his neck back just like his father used to do, "You think so, too?"

"Yeah," I fearfully responded in shame, rubbing my palms together, "Crazy."

Martin shook his head in disagreement, smiling at the same time. The guilt is overwhelming me. I turned to look my child in the eyes, took him under my arm and planted a kiss on his forehead.

"Come on, Mom, you got that lipstick on me," he scolded as he used his hand to scrub away my lasting mark of love.

"Hush, boy."

He gave me a hug and rubbed my back, "Everything happens for a reason."

"You always say that, son," I expressed, "God is going to bless you for sure."

I nodded and pondered on whether I should tell him about the letter Rodney wrote me. Before I could, Rodney hung out the front door and handed off the phone to Martin.

"It's Everett."

Martin took hold of the phone and continued his conversation inside. I finished my morning smoke and went inside right behind him to begin cleaning the kitchen. I could hear bits and pieces of what my child was saying to Everett. Honestly, the hostility in his voice had me worried.

"Mom," I turned to face Martin standing directly behind me, "We're leaving."

"Okay, heed to the warning and watch your surroundings, son."

"We will."

"Later Ms. Stacy," Rodney added.

The boys raced down the street to catch the bus on the corner. Luckily, we only stayed a couple of blocks away. On the way Martin questioned Rodney.

"Do you like my Mom, Rod?"

He sat in shock then broke the silence with a chuckle. Martin's face was scrunched up and irritated.

"It's nothing like that, bro I honestly don't know how to feel."

Martin smiled, then asked again, "Do you like my, Mom?"

"No," the smile immediately left Rodney's face, "I love your Mom."

Martin rubbed his head and glared out the window for a moment. He brushed his faded hair forward then brought his attention back to Rodney. Martin's teeth clinched, gritting in deep frustration as he licked his lips just before they parted.

"...my mom has been hurt a lot in her life, man," Martin expressed.

"I just want her to know that whatever happens I'm there for..."

"It doesn't matter, Rod," Martin cut in, "I'm trusting you."

Although Rodney wanted to, he never mentioned the note. He didn't want to say or do anything else to make Martin upset. So, for the rest of the ride they sat in silence. The boys arrived at the bus station and noticed a clutter of people surrounding a pile of commotion.

"Everett!" Martin exclaimed, "Come on, Rod!"

They each rushed off the bus and pushed their way through the crowd of people. Through all the commotion Martin was still able to notice a few familiar faces as well as Reggie, but no Everett. Martin jumped in with the first blow and Rodney right after that. They were amid the fight, afflicting much damage. The other boys were outnumbered. One by one they peeled back and ran off.

"Martin!"

Reggie pushed through the crowd to get to Rodney and Martin. As they were still throwing punches and lunging at suspicious folks. Reggie snatched Martin by the shoulder to get his attention.

"Where is, Everett?" Reggie questioned, "I told him to run to the payphone and call the twins."

"He told us to come quick," Martin explained, "I don't know where the twins went."

Reggie sighed and scratched his head, "He called me an hour ago and said he'd be down here waiting."

Martin questioned, "Where was he?"

Reggie tried to catch his breath before speaking, "Grabbing from that crazy fool, Omar."

"Big homie, Omar?" Rodney questioned confused.

"It's a setup!" Martin exclaimed.

Another bus pulled in slow, "We got to get on this bus, and it'll drop us right in the back of Omar's."

"Does Omar know where you live now?" Reggie questioned Rodney.

"If he does, he didn't find out from me," Rodney confessed, "Honest."

"We need to hurry up and get over there," Martin urged, "Get on the bus!"

By the time they got to Omar's, Everett was neck and neck with Omar and his younger brother Donny in the backyard. When the bus slowed to a stop each of the boys rushed off and ran over to aid Everett. There were six of them. Though, every one of Reggie's boys piled on the bus with them.

"What's up Reggie," Donny threatened, "They can't save you."

They still outnumbered Omar and his boys. Reggie and Donny went toe to toe. Reggie rushed Donny picked him up and slammed him down on the concrete.

"5-O!" One of the boys screamed.

Reggie threw one last punch before they all scattered like roaches. At least thirty kids scattered from the commotion. There were so many people that the police turned on their lights and loud speakers. Like cattle, the crowd moved from side to side up and down alleyways. East Denver was full of alleys Reggie, Martin and Rodney were able to stop and crouch down on the side of a dumpster.

"Go home and let your brothers know what's going on Martin, I'm going back to look for Everett," Reggie told him, "Go straight home!"

"What if you can't find him?" Martin asked, "Everybody else dipped."

Reggie began to jog away, "go home, Martin," he said in the distance.

Martin was afraid, he figured if Reggie went back alone then Omar and Donny will jump on him. All the other boys are most likely hiding in other nooks and cranny's around Omar's house. Martin hoped that Everett was with one of them.

"Damn, man," he threw punches at an old fence.

"Martin," Rodney hesitated, "I didn't tell anybody anything, they must've seen me going inside or something."

### (SIRENS)

"Come on man the blocks hot," Martin told him, "Let's get out of here."

They didn't make it home for another hour and a half. By now, it's three o'clock in the afternoon. Rodney and Martin walked up to the door and rang the bell.

"You got your key?"

"Nah, I left it in my other pants," Rodney replied.

Chane rushed to the door and snatched it open, "What happened?"

"Reggie called, bro, we got to hurry up and get back down there...Omar is on some funk for real," Martin told him.

I heard Martin and Rodney as they came into the house. Corey ran up the stairs from the basement with his Glock in hand.

"Where did you and Corey go," Martin questioned.

"We had to make a pickup, bro."

"We're sitting pretty now," Corey added, hoisting his gun up.

"Tell me what happened, Martin!" Chane asked.

"Everett got jumped, Reggie and his boys met us at Downing," Martin spat, as he punched his fist into his palm, "We all get on the bus, boom, we get to Omar's and then 5-O came."

"Nah, let's go Chane," Corey coaxed, "We about to get the stolio and smash down there, guns blazing!"

"I'm going!" Martin told them.

"Me too," Rodney added, "This is my fault."

I could hear them loud talking about guns and blazing up. I couldn't just lay in bed, so I jumped up and dashed into the front room.

"What's going on?" I said in a panic, "What are you boys doing?"

"Mom, calm down, everything's okay," Martin assured me.

"I can hear you from my bedroom!" I yelled, "Nobody leave this house! I mean it!"

"We have to go, Mom," Corey told me, "You want the problem at the house again?"

Of course, I don't want that at all. I also don't want the boys to go out looking for trouble. I didn't respond.

"Then, we'll see you when it's taken care of," Corey said.

"Don't you dare disrespect me!" I screamed, "I'll be dead before you disrespect me, boy."

I glared down and noticed the gun in Corey's grip. He was holding onto the damn thing so tight if he would've sneezed, boom. If I punch him right in the kisser now, he wouldn't have a moment to squeeze and blast. I'm so mad, I could just take the gun and shoot off my baby's toe myself.

"Mom," Chane softly called out to me, as he took me by the hand leading me back into my room, "We have to go."

"Give me my cigarettes damnit!" I snatched away and made my way onto the front porch.

"Come on, Corey," Chane coaxed, "We'll go down the alley."

"Go get on the bus and hurry up," Corey told Rodney and Martin.

I know that the twins want to protect their younger brother, but I want to protect the twins. The twins get into far more trouble than Martin or Rodney together. I think. I know what I'm talking about. I know my kids! I wiped my tears as I took long pulls of my cigarette. I needed more than one I was so frustrated. I was in deep thought when I heard the door open and slowly shut behind me.

"Ms. Stacy, can I sit with you?" a soft deep voice spoke.

I turned and glanced up to see Rodney peering over me, "Sure, honey."

"Did you like it," he asked.

I was silently confused for a moment, "Oh, the poem it was beautiful, Rodney."

"Thank you, I was working on it all day yesterday…I was too scared to give it to you."

He began to fidget with his hands, "Don't be nervous I will not judge you…I want you to be able to tell me anything."

Rodney gazed into my eyes, "...I knew you were up because you turned off the television after your show went off..."

I wasn't surprised or shocked. I remember to understand that every moment of the day he is still a stranger. Although, he doesn't scare me anymore. I turned my attention to Sam pulling into the driveway. Rodney quickly stood up to rush back in the house. Just before he got out of the car with a bright smile.

"Rodney," I called out just before the door shut tightly behind him.

"Honey, I'm home," Sam joked.

I sighed, "Hey, babe."

Sam made his way up the driveway to me. The closer he got the more he noticed how unhappy I seemed.

"What's wrong, love, where's the boys?"

He planted a kiss upon my forehead, then stood by and waited for my response.

"They're all inside getting ready to leave...they got into some trouble today, Sam," I cried, "They won't tell me, but I know they're about to do something crazy."

Tears rolled down my cheeks as Martin scurried out the front door.

"Pop, pop we got to go now!" he blurted out, "The twins!"

"What's going on, son?"

"I'll explain in the car, we got to go."

"Let me go get my shoes," I said in a panic.

Sam shook his head in disagreement, "No Stacy! Stay here...it's just me and my boys."

"What am I supposed to do?" I hollered, "Sit here and wait for God knows what to happen!"

Sam pointed at me and in a serious tone he said, "Stay here."

"Rodney!" Martin shouted, "Come on!"

"Get in the car boys," Sam directed them.

Rodney zipped out the door past me, "I'm coming."

I watched in dread with my jaw dropped as they quickly drove away. They tell me everything except for what I need to know. I'm praying that it doesn't turn midnight and I didn't receive a call. Or worse, nobody phoned home, and nobody came back home to me either. After about twenty minutes of some well needed alone time I went back inside. I didn't know what to do I stayed in the kitchen and the family room pacing back and forth. Like I'm fifteen all over again, depressed because I can't stop thinking about what I need to do. Though, once again, there is nothing that I can do at all. One hour had gone by like it was one entire day. The time was just dragging on and my patients was wearing thin. So much so, I finished off my last ten cigarettes. Once, three hours passed and the skies darkened I knew it wasn't going to be good. I sprawled out on the couch and listened to the ticking clock in the darkness.

*(Phone Rings)*

I damn near jumped out of my skin trying to get to the phone, "Hello."

"Mom, mom he's dead...they shot him, he's dead," Martin whaled on the other end.

My heart sank into my stomach and the feeling of

terror loomed over me. Martin was on the other end of the phone crying hysterically. He was so hysterical I could barely understand him. I was praying that I understood him wrong.

"Martin, baby…son," I called out to him as tears began crowding my vision, "Who?"

"Chane!" He shouted, then let out a deep groan.

I dropped the phone and plummeted to the floor. I clawed and banged on the ground as if it were to blame. I rolled onto my side and gasped for air, my mouth was wide open. Though, no noise was coming out. In my distraught and hopeless state, I crawled into the kitchen slid across the tiles to the icebox, grabbed one of Sam's beers and slammed it. Before it was even finished I tossed the bottle across the room and grabbed another.

Martin and Rodney arrived home without Sam. They walked into the front door and were immediately greeted by broken beer bottles and me in a drunken stoop on the kitchen floor.

"Mom," Martin called out to me, "Mom, get up."

I opened my eyes only to be faced with Martin and Rodney covered in blood. My eyes widened in terror as I screamed at the top of my lungs. I felt them hoisting me up from the ground, but I couldn't get balanced. I found my footing and snatched Martin out of his blood red clothes. I snatched at Rodney, but I was only able to get him out of his jacket. The three of us went out into the alley and set the clothes on fire. We stood by watching the flames.

"Where's your father?" I questioned, concerned.

"I don't know," Martin replied softly.

# The Funeral

"We are joined here today to celebrate the life of Chane Christopher Jacobs a brother, a son, a loving young man, and a caring friend," Pastor Porter began.

The church was full of the boys' friends and members of their families. Dominic, my mother, Terry and my Grandmother were my only support. Of course, Sam's entire family showed up. There were so many people yet few seats. Lined up along the walls and standing so far as the doorway. These young riff raffs were mixed in together setting all feuds aside in honor of my son, a great friend.

Pastor Porter continued, "Chane was what some would call intelligent, but what I would call wise...he did as he was told by his mother Stacy Viera-Jacobs and by his father Samuel Michael Jacobs he cared

about and looked out for his brothers and friends…
but now, may he watch over us peacefully in heaven."

Pastor said a few more good words then allowed
Martin to take the stand. He glanced out over the
crowd before his lips parted and he finally spoke.

"There's not much I really can say except this was
my brother…he held me in his arms when I was first
given life…and I held him in my arms when his life
was taken away," Martin wowed the crowd.

I burst into tears as I listened to what my baby boy
had to say about his brother.

"My brother was truly an angel in disguise, he
supported me when I needed it the most…he did what
a big brother was supposed to do…he showed me the
ropes, so that one day…I can be wise like him."

Martin left the stand. He gave his brother one
last kiss and seated himself beside me. Corey was
the next to take the stand. He went up with Rodney
and began with a sudden burst of emotion, though
Rodney held him up and urged him to take the stand.

"This was my brother, this was my twin, my other
half…now a part of me is dead," Corey said holding
back the tears. "Bullets don't have a name on them."

There was so much more that Corey wanted to
say. He placed his head in his palm and sulked for a
moment, resting over the pastors stand. Rodney and
Corey left the stand then Sam and I were the next in
line. He's been away from home ever since Chane
was killed. Sam wrapped his arm around me and
adjusted the microphone to my height.

"That's my son right there…Sam and I tried
to do our best to raise our children the right way.
Obviously, we needed a little more time…they could

be better," I said, "It's not easy for me as a mother, to see my child like this …but, I know he'll always be with us in spirit."

Sam's sister, Annette, took the stand right after us. That woman got up there and cried like a Llama in labor. She wasn't talking or anything. Honestly, before Sam pulled her down, folks were looking at me like I didn't love Chane as much as she had. To our surprise Rodney had a few words to say at the last moment.

"Chane was like a big brother to me even though I'm older by one year…he and his family took me in, bought me clothes, shoes, fed me, and gave me love… and I never got to thank him…thank you, Chane."

He slowly made his way to the casket and kissed Chane's forehead.

"Save me a place," he whispered.

The choir sang a song and the pastor spoke to the youth about their affiliations in gangs. He spoke about violence, peace, making a name for ourselves and making a difference. It was a powerful message that I am praying everyone heard.

"God is watching," Pastor Porter said, then wrapped up the service.

Coming home wasn't easy, after a few members of the family left the silence broke each of us down.

"I want my brother man I need him here it will never be the same without him," Martin cried out.

He passed the bottle of vodka to Rodney, "What you want to do?"

"Man, what you think?" Martin shouted, "I'm not letting this go."

"I'm right here with you," Rodney assured him, "Whatever you want to do."

Corey listened from the other side of the screen door, he was interested in what the conversation pertained to, and if it pertained to Chane he needed to be a part of it.

"You don't have a choice...you're a part of this family too, now...right?" Corey spoke out from the darkness.

Rodney slowly nodded in agreement, "Right."

Corey cautiously stepped over to Rodney, his hands in his pockets and a face full of sorrow. Rodney passed on the bottle to Corey. Corey nodded smiling with joyous tears and took a swig of vodka.

"I don't blame you," Corey spoke, "You know that?"

Rodney dropped his head and sulked to himself. Each of the boys banded together and shed their painful tears as a unit.

# Moving On

It's been a year since Chane passed on. Life is almost the same with the company of Rodney, seeing as he is Chane's keeper. The investigation into Chane's murder is still open. At first, school was tough for the boys, seeing students walking around with T-shirts made for Chane, poems and so many other things people did to show they loved Chane. I allowed them to go back when they were ready. So, second semester began the beginning of the school year for my boys. The whole school seemed to sympathize for them, as they tried to go on normally. Martin was dating a beautiful girl named, Natasha Blue. She was a down to earth girl and undenounced to me had been friends with Martin since elementary. They even shared a first kiss. What they had together was truly special.

"Hey, babe," Natasha greeted him in the hall just before lunch.

Martin planted a kiss on her lips, "Hey, what's up."

"What are we eating for lunch? It's my treat," she said with pride.

"I don't care," Martin said, "Rodney's coming up here, he got some fire if you want to smoke?"

Natasha poked out her hip and crossed her arms over her chest, "Don't ask a question you already know the answer to."

They laughed as Natasha's older sister Keisha had come down the hall tucked under Rodney's arm.

"They let you in, bro," Martin questioned Rodney.

"I just walked in," Rodney responded, "They still think I'm a student."

"Can we smoke first or eat?" Keisha asked, "Or something?"

"Well, let's smoke first," Martin suggested, "Munchies!"

The four of them made their way through the crowded halls and out the front doors to the crowded bus stop. It might as well be the smoking section. Out of well over forty people maybe two got on the bus. The goal was to smoke, get on the bus to get food and then come back late from lunch.

"I want you to come to my house tonight, babe," Martin offered.

Natasha smiled, "Meeting parents makes me nervous."

Martin chuckled, "My mom will love you...my pops, too."

Keisha and Rodney stood behind the bus bench, blocking the wind and preparing to spark up the blunt.

"Let me spark this one, sexy," Keisha flirted.

"For what?" Rodney snapped, "It's coming to you."

In a cute, innocent voice, "You sparked the last one."

"Alright, damn, here."

The four of them watched a few buses go by until the blunt died out. They boarded the bus headed west to a familiar place. They sat in their regular booth by the window and made fun of the people passing by. After devouring their meals, they all together dashed to the bus and headed back to school. Martin couldn't wait until the bell rang. The four of them came together again.

"So, are you coming to the house?" Martin asked Natasha.

She struggled to jam large textbooks inside of the thin locker. Martin stood by laughing.

"Yeah, let me find Keisha and we'll meet at the bus stop, okay."

The bus ride was extremely hot, crowded and tiring. Upon entering the house, Martin seated the girls in the living room.

"Momma!" he ran through the house screaming.

I stood in the kitchen peering over at the girls laughing as they watched Martin run up and down the hall screaming my name. Finally, he came back out into the living room and noticed me standing there.

"How long you been right there?" Martin asked.

I laughed, "Long enough."

"Mom, this is Natasha and her sister Keisha," He announced. "Natasha is my girl."

"It's nice to meet the two of you."

"You too," they replied in unison.

Martin took the girls into the backyard space and seated them comfortably. Keisha pulled snacks from her bag and randomly tossed them. Her number one target, Rodney. Snacks bounced off him until he'd had enough.

"Stop playing, Keisha!" Rodney complained, "Do you have a lighter, Martin?"

Martin and Natasha laughed from across the room. He fondled around in his pockets.

"Hold on let me go find one," Rodney offered.

He handed off the half of blunt to Keisha and dashed inside. I stood in the kitchen reading today's paper, waiting for Sam to get back with Corey. Lately, Sam and Corey have been off doing their own thing. I'm afraid to ask them what. Rodney walked in and planted a moist kiss on my cheek.

"Do you have a lighter, Mom?" I dug into my shirt and brought the lighter from my bra.

"Bring it back to me."

Rodney kissed my cheek again then rushed back outside. He was back with my lighter just seconds later, "Here you go, Mom."

We exchanged a smile before he left my presence once again. Rodney stepped out in the backyard and took a seat next to Keisha. She captured his attention and planted a moist kiss on his lips.

"Are you taking me to prom this year?" Keisha asked confidently.

"I don't know I don't feel like dressing down," he responded in a boring tone.

Keisha smacked her lips, "I don't want to have to go by myself, Rodney."

I came to the door with the phone, "Martin, baby, it's your brother."

"Thanks, mom…what it is," he said into the phone.

"Martin, go in the basement," Corey muttered.

Martin stepped inside and went into the dark, damp basement, "Okay, what's up bro, what's going on?"

"Do me a favor," Corey continued, "In the corner behind the speaker get my gun wrap it in a towel or a shirt and bring it outside inside of a shoebox or something, do it now."

Martin got the gun from behind the speaker and unloaded the clip. He checked to make sure that there was no bullet in the chamber. Martin wiped away his finger prints and wrapped the gun up with the towel. He grabbed a shoe box from Corey's closet and placed the towel inside. Martin rushed upstairs and outside to the car. He got into the backseat and handed the box off to Corey.

"What's going on, Dad?"

Sam sighed, "Your brother has some business to take care of, son, this has nothing to do with you, go inside."

Martin sat silent as he stared at the back of Sam's head.

"Come back home, bro."

Martin placed his hand on Corey's shoulder. A tear fell from Corey's eye as he slowly turned to glance into his baby brothers' worried face.

"I'm not going to leave you Martin, but I can't let this ride."

Martin wrapped his arm around Corey and held

on tight for a while. He slowly left the backseat of the car and watched as they quickly drove away. Corey and Sam reached the stop sign then made a right. Martin came back inside and ran straight for the backyard.

"Pops and Corey just left."

"Where'd they go," Rodney asked.

Martin slowly sat down next to Natasha and looked up at Rodney, "They turned right."

Martin and Rodney each sat in awe for a few minutes. Unaware of what was happening the girls awkwardly giggled.

"Natasha, you have to go," Martin finally spoke.

Natasha straightened up, "Why?"

"I'll tell you later."

On the short walk to the bus stop Martin didn't say a word to Natasha. Every question she asked he searched for the answers on the pavement. Natasha grew anxious she took him by the arm and stopped him in his tracks.

"Martin," she whined, "say something to me, babe, I'm worried about you."

Martin sighed, "It's nothing, Tasha."

Martin smiled and kissed her cheek attempting to mask his nervousness, he continued to walk. They waited at the bus stop silently for just a few minutes until the bus arrived. On the walk back to the house Martin still had nothing at all to say. The boys went straight to the backyard.

"What happened?" Rodney questioned right away, "What did Corey say?"

"He came to get the burner and I watched them

drive down the street...they went right toward Omar's," Martin dropped his head in his palms.

Rodney glared at the floor, "Let's..."

The sliding door flung open. He was interrupted by Corey coming out onto the patio swiftly.

"Damn! Damn! Damn!" Corey repeated.

"What happened? Tell me what's up!" Martin demanded.

Corey took a seat and lit up a cigarette. Inhaling and exhaling the smoke with disdain. Rodney and Martin sat silent eager to know what just took place. They watched as he rapidly tapped his foot and puffed several times. Sam hung out the back door and gestured for Corey to follow him back inside. He handed off the cigarette to Rodney and quickly ran in.

"What you think happened?" Martin asked in disbelief.

"I'm with you on this one," Rodney replied puzzled, throwing his hands in the air.

Corey returned gripping a white tall T shirt in his palm. His eyes were deep red, and his teeth clutched as he tossed the shirt into Martin's face. Rodney stood to his feet then rushed over to snatch the shirt away. He held it open, revealing large areas of blood splatter. Corey pulled the gun from his pants and opened the once full clip. There were no more bullets. Rodney tossed the shirt onto Martin.

"Emptied the clip," he paused, "I put every one of them bullets in Omar!"

Martin tossed the shirt back to Corey and a moment of silence fell upon them.

"That's Omar's blood?" Rodney questioned.

Corey took a second to reply. He brushed his waves forward and ran his hand down his face as he nodded his head slowly in agreeance and sighed.

"What if the T's come, bro?"

"Damn! Don't bring that up, dude, for real!" Corey argued, "They weren't doing nothing about it."

Corey sounded so upset and I was curious to know why, so I stood in the doorway of the patio. The boys had no idea how long I had been there, just listening, horrified. Rodney glanced up at me then quickly kicked the bloody shirt into the corner. Martin jumped up from his seat looking to Corey. Corey sat quietly unaffected. As if nothing were wrong he took a few more swigs of the vodka glared up at me and shrugged his shoulders.

"It's over."

The look on my baby boy's face sent a chill down my spine and a shock through my body so intense I began to shake. There were so many things going through my mind that my mouth was ready to speak but couldn't. I lost my breath and my voice was literally gone. My body went completely numb and I could barely feel a thing. I literally died on the inside.

"I did what I had to do," Corey declared, "I did what my brother would have done for me."

"Murder, Corey!" I cried aloud, confused.

I thought that I would die if I just broke down right there. I know exactly who to go after, Sam.

"Sam!" I screamed through the house, "Sam!"

Corey stared at the floor in shame. Rodney flinched at my blood curdling screams in disbelief as Martin fell to his knees and began to pray repeatedly.

Sam cautiously stepped out the bedroom and into the hall.

"Why are you screaming?" He questioned, pretending to be clueless, "What's wrong with you?"

I ran at top speed down the hall toward him. Punching, slapping and kicking him, anything I could to inflict damage. I scratched at his face and pounded on his head repeatedly as he ducked down and blocked the blows. Martin raced into the back hall with us trying to stop me from harming his Dad.

"Mom, no stop!" He begged.

Sam yelled out in anguish, "Stacy!"

"I hate you!"

I repeated over and over as I threw blow after blow. Martin tugged onto my arms trying to pull me back. So, I took hold of the back of Sam's collar and pulled back as well. The three of us fell to the floor. One on top or over the other. Still, I punched and kicked at Sam with all the force in my petite body.

"Stacy! Calm down!" Sam screamed. "Calm down, Stacy!"

Sam scrambled to his feet and dashed into our bedroom.

"Get out!" I yelled, wriggling away from Martin's grasp, "I hate you!"

Once I rose to my feet, Sam was ready to leave with his keys and a light jacket. He stood toe to toe with me as Martin and Rodney stood close behind, trying to stop the fight. The minute I raised my hand to Sam he wrapped his arms around me, lifted me up high and slammed my body to the ground. The entire house shook. Rodney and Corey finally intervened and broke up the fight. Sam punched a hole in the bedroom door and rushed out of the house, slamming the door shut behind him.

"Mom," Corey aided me, "Are you okay?"

"Get off of me!"

I threw on a coat, a pair of sneakers then snatched up my keys and cigarettes. Before I could get the door open I could hear Sam ripping out of the drive-way. Rodney watched from the family room as I stormed out in total shock. I drove all around town before stopping in Aurora to visit my mother. After a few hours I began to get calls from the house back to back. I assumed it was just Sam calling to see when I'd be home, so I ignored them. Besides, I was just minutes away from home when he called for the last time. When I turned onto my street all I seen was blinding bright lights and a huge crowd of silhouettes. The Police Department was about seven to eight cars deep. Surrounding my house blocking my alley way and my front yard. I quickly parked and jetted over to my house through the large crowd. Inside, I found Sam handcuffed on the couch with a gun to his head and a pissed cop ready to pull the trigger.

"Wait!" I pleaded with the officer.

"Ma'am, please step back your husband is under arrest for homicide," the officer informed me, "We're taking him into custody."

"Stacy, take the boys out on the patio."

The boys watched from the kitchen window as the officer placed Sam in the back of the squad car. They drove away with Sam's eyes locked onto my soaked face mouthing the words 'I love you,' to me. My boys and I stood in amazement as the squad car disappeared further into the distance.

# Unresolved

Corey and Rodney are helping me to come up with the money that we need to pay the bills. Martin's doing what he needs to be doing at school. Every day, since the arrest, has been harder and harder on us. I haven't got on Corey about the murder yet because I'm not sure how to approach a murderer. Now, this man that I raised from a boy is a stranger to me. I sat out on the patio with my cigarette lit and drink in hand. *Sigh* My son is not a murderer, I don't know what to call him. Just not a that! I was sure that I was home alone until Corey stood in the doorway. It seems like every time he walks into the room it sends chills rushing all through my body. Now, I'm convinced that he carries the same pint of vodka around every day. I really want to say something to him. I know I really need to.

"Hey, mom," Corey mumbled over my shoulder.

"Hey, son," whimpering to myself I replied, frail.

"Is it alright for me to sit down?"

I took a drag of my cigarette as I nodded my head in agreeance noticeably. Corey took a seat, sipped his liquor bottle and quietly stared me down. I guess looking at him wouldn't have killed me, but my perceptions of him were too strong. If I look at him then I must remember that I love him. In remembering that I love him I can't ever forget that he will take someone's life, and that is not what God intends.

"It's time for me to move around," he said, "You can't even look at me."

For the first time in days, my son and I locked eyes. Anger, sadness, confusion and everything in between I could feel. The tears wouldn't leave my eyes as if I don't have any more tears left inside of me. The bags underneath Corey's eyes revealed to me how stressed out he seemed to be, too.

"What do you mean, son?"

"I need to leave I caused too much, shit."

Reluctant, I asked, "Is someone going to come after you?"

Corey dropped his head into his lap. Now, I don't want him here I don't want a murderer in my home. Keeping in mind that he is my seed is the only thing keeping me sane and keeping the love alive. With the last bit of love, I have for my own damn child, I got up from my seat and held my baby. I stroked his head and reassured him that I am at least still his mother.

"I will never let you go, I will never let you down, or allow you to be taken from me...you're my child, no matter how big you get you are still my baby! No matter what you do."

His tears soaked the sleeve of my shirt, "I'm sorry, Mom."

"I love you, Corey, I'm your mother and this is your home here with me and your family. You don't have to go!" I pleaded.

After all the years of raising them I've never got in the way of whatever it was my children attempted to pursue. Whether or not it was good or bad for them, I let them learn for themselves just how life can be. Most of the time it worked in my favor, though Corey's idea of leaving seems to be certain to work out for him. I know it will work for me. I hope it works. One minute I can look at him and then the next minute I don't want him here.

"Where are you going to go?" I asked, doubting that he will leave.

"Grandma let me know she's got space for me in Aurora I can walk around with no worries and get a job."

My jaw dropped in awe. All the painful years I spent trying to get out of her presence I would have never guessed one of my babies would be fighting so hard to go back. I never told my boys about my moms' old ways I haven't told them much about my past. Although I didn't agree, I did not stray Corey away from the idea. I believe he knows what's best for himself. I grabbed my son by the hand and led him inside.

"I want to at least try it out," Corey explained, making his way into the dining room.

"Okay, baby, when did you want to go?" I questioned, plopping down on the sofa.

"Grandma's on her way right now," he filled me in.

### (Doorbell Rings)

I quickly got up to answer the door, "How long ago did you talk to her?" I asked.

Corey glared up at me with a puzzled expression, "Not that long."

I scramble over to the front door. A middle-aged white male wielding a suitcase greeted me with a smile. I propped open the screen door as he climbed up the porch steps. Corey glanced past me, vastly got up and retreated to the basement to pack his things.

"Hi, how are you?"

"Hi, are you Stacy Jacobs?" The man asked.

My heart is telling me that this has something to do with my boys. My mind is telling me that this absolutely has something to do with one of my boys.

"Yes, and you are?"

"I'm a detective here to ask you a few questions about your husband Mr. Samuel Jacobs."

"Please, come in." I invited.

"Thank you, ma'am."

The man removed his hat and proceeded inside where we gathered into the kitchen. I poured the man a nice glass of cold ice water from the fridge.

"Have a seat," I gestured to the table.

"Thank you. Mrs. Jacobs, I am Detective Ryan Moss," he began, "I'm sure you are aware of your husband's pending case, correct?"

"Yes, sir," I replied, avoiding further details.

"Had you noticed any strange behavior in your husband lately, anything that may have been out of the ordinary, anything unfamiliar?"

I nervously rubbed my palms together before responding.

"No, for the most part, he went to work came home and watched the set."

The detective revealed to me two photographs of Sam's car.

"Is this your husband's vehicle?"

"Yes, sir," I responded confidently.

"I have reason to believe your husband's vehicle is connected to multiple homicides."

My heart can't take any more blows. At this rate, I'm going to have a mental breakdown. I nodded my head there was nothing more that I could say. At this point, I'm truly amazed I had no damn idea. How could I be so blind? I don't put anything past anybody, certainly not murder past Sam. I'm convinced he was capable of many more things. It takes me back to the night the beatings stopped. I had never seen Sam so afraid in my life he really thought he should've died. Now, I wonder what was really going on with him?

The officer pulled two more pictures from his briefcase.

"I'm going to show you these photos and I want you to tell me if you recognize either of the men."

In the first photo, the detective revealed to me a bald man, with a strong build. The second looked similar to the first. Though, a little older and lighter in his complexion. Somewhat like mine.

"They aren't familiar faces," I responded swabbing the tears from my face.

"Okay, keep your eyes open for these two," he warned, "They deal in money laundering something else I think your husband may have gotten into. Any ideas on that?"

Detective Moss looked about the house from his seat. My eyes following his, as he scanned our belongings. He can see for himself that we aren't poor.

"Sir, I'm sure if he had big money he'd move us out of this place down to Cherry Creek or some other much nicer place," I scoffed, "hell I wouldn't be busting my ass at work every damn day I can tell you that."

"We've conducted a full search of the vehicle and truthfully ma'am *Sigh*…with everything we found in the vehicle there is no need to search the home, unless something else comes to our attention, of course."

Every nerve in my body is trembling. I was terribly curious to know what was found in the car, though I didn't want to ask any suspicious questions. Detective Moss collected the photos and placed them back in his brief case. Luckily, he made his visit brief as well. Martin and Rodney came striding up to the porch from Martin's school. They each made their way inside and straight into the kitchen to give me a hug and kiss.

"Hey, Mom."

"Hey," Martin chimed in, still holding onto me.

Rodney left the kitchen and proceeded to the basement where Corey was packing his things.

Martin glared at Detective Moss from over my shoulders.

"Who are you?"

"I'm Detective Ryan Moss, son, I came by to ask your mother a few questions," he responded as he rose to his feet.

Martin firmly shook his hand and left the kitchen. I shook Mr. Moss' hand as well, then led him to the door.

"I've talked to Mr. Jacobs personally and in my honest opinion he seems to be a stand-up guy," Detective Moss said in an attempt to lift my spirits, "I can almost assure you that there will be a subpoena to bring you forth as a witness, although I'm sure this will not go to trial, he's already confessed."

I smiled and fell back into thought as tears streamed down my face. Detective Moss turned the knob of the screen door then doubled back just before leaving.

"He had an accomplice in the murder of Omar Wright, there was a driver and an assailant shooting," he informed me. "Though, he claims he was alone."

I damn near collapsed when he brought up the accomplice thing on me. I knew who he was talking about and I'm sure he's got to have some idea that Sam has talked to me about all this. Although, we truly haven't. Nothing was ever said between us each time something went down with him or the boys. They leave me totally clueless. I wonder where I am when all this stuff is going on. Maybe stuck inside of my puny mind pondering about nothing!

"It's been a pleasure meeting you and I'm sure we

will be talking again, Mrs. Jacobs," Detective Moss stated.

When he said that it alarmed me, of course, there were other witnesses. If there were I hope they don't know Corey. From what I know about my boys, there are multiple people who can and probably will identify Corey. The detective gave me his card and allowed me access to his assistance anytime of the day or night. As he pulled away from the house my mother was arriving.

"Corey, Grandma Terry is here

I slipped on some shoes, grabbed my cigarettes and strolled out the front door onto the porch.

"Damn, bro," Martin expressed.

"Do you really have to leave?" Rodney asked curiously.

"It's just better, this way," Corey stated, "The trouble will follow me."

"I'm sure," Martin joked, "The trouble will target the house, stupid."

"Damn!" Rodney exclaimed.

"Help me with these bags," Corey murmured sadly.

The boys picked up whatever they could handle and carted out Corey's things to their Grandma Terry's car.

"Are you going to be okay, Stacy?" my mother asked deeply concerned.

I took a drag of my cigarette and pulled Rodney and Martin underneath each arm, "We'll be just fine."

"Okay, if you need anything at all just call," My mother assured me.

I let my boys go turned away and rushed into

my house broken hearted. Corey took a deep breath before getting in the car and shutting the door to leave. I completely broke down before solemnly agreeing with myself that my happy family is falling apart. I'm so fed up with tussling over the two major changes that just occurred in my life today. I smoked a blunt to myself and fell into a glorious slumber.

A few hours later I woke up to darkness and silence. I stretched out on my bed and felt a mass sitting just at the edge. I swiftly sat up, but to my surprise it was Rodney there watching me.

"It's okay, Mom," He whispered, "it's just me."

"Boy," I leaned back on the pillows took a deep breath and sighed, "Where is Corey and Martin?"

"Corey's gone to Grandma Terry's, remember?" he questioned.

I ran my fingers through my hair glaring at the ceiling as all the memoirs of the day rushed back to me. Once again, I began to cry. Rodney cautiously climbed up into my bed above my covers and held me in his arms. He laid his head on my breast while looking up at me whipping the tears from my eyes.

"It's okay, Momma."

Rodney paused, before carrying on he glared into my eyes. I ran my knuckles across his cheek messaging his face. He really does look just like my boys, as if he were all three of them combined into one. I sat up in my lush blankets and propped against my fluffy pillows trying to relax my mind. Rodney swiftly sat up allowing me to move. All at once, a cry left from deep within me.

"I'm sorry, son," I cried with my back to him, "Go on out of here."

Rodney scurried out the door and back to the room that he shared with Martin. Rodney shut the door behind him and soundlessly climbed back into his bed. Martin's eyes were wide open, he sat up and twisted his body around to face Rodney glaring back at him.

"What happened?" Martin scolded.

Rodney sat in silence across the room before finally parting his lips

"Nothing," Rodney answered, "I was just checking to make sure Mom was, okay."

Martin chuckled at the very thought, he smiled in the dark and the anger began to dissolve into delight as he listened to a true friend express his heart felt emotions.

"I love her," Rodney said blissful.

"I love my mama, too," Martin said giggling, tucking himself away for the night, "Goodnight, bro."

"Goodnight, bro and I apologize," he explained, "no disrespect."

"We straight," Martin said, yawning, "We have to make sure Mom is straight, too."

# Sentencing Day

Today, Sam is being sentenced for killing Omar. Omar's family was not very big at all. There was joy in witnessing the conviction of my son's murderer. Though, I never prayed for his death to fill the void. Omar wasn't necessarily a kid I'm sure, but he was still someone's child. My sympathy ran very deep for the young boy. Corey, Martin and Rodney sat in the row behind my mother and I, gossiping in a silent undertone.

"There goes that dude that came to the house."

Martin said pointing to the left side of the court room at Detective Moss. I quickly stole a glance and noticed him, too. Strange, he's seated in the crowd. I thought he would be on the stand or something. He never did come back.

"Who?" Rodney questioned.

"The detective," Martin responded.

I turned to face the boys, "Quiet."

I swiveled back around Just as Sam entered the courtroom.

"Here he comes," My mother whispered.

Tears flowed as I stretch my neck over two rows of large heads. Trying desperately to get a glance at my loving husband in chains and too far from my reach. Sam approached the stand with a very rugged look that I hadn't seen since his goon days. Though, I've never desired him so much in my life. Craving for his touch with such drive I burst into tears.

"Sam," I whispered beneath my shaken breath.

"Mr. Jacobs, you are being convicted for the murder of twenty-year old Omar Wright, what is your plea?" the judge asked of him.

"Guilty."

That was the only thing I heard from Sam as he stood before the judge confident, his chest out and his feet planted. Sam turned to look back at me gazing at him. When he smiled, I drowned out everything and everyone around me. He blew a kiss to me in mid-air, and I blew one right back. Sam hung his head low and slowly turned his body back to facing the judge amid explaining his sentence.

"I am hereby sentencing you to forty years imprisonment in the Colorado department of Corrections with no possibility of parole," the judge lectured.

My body went cold, my legs grew weak as my arms got numb. Shortness of breath got me lightheaded when I stood to speak out, I collapsed to the ground. Everyone in the court room gasped at once, a hush fell over the crowd and my sons rushed to pick my lifeless body up from the ground. Two officers lead Sam away, though he kept his eye on us until we were out of view. Minutes later, my eyes opened to my three boys and my mother surrounding me in fear. They each desperately hoped that I would have opened my eyes just before Sam had to leave the courtroom. For his own assurance in knowing that I was okay. My family helped me to my feet, and we left realizing Sam is not coming home with us. We hung our heads with teary eyes on our way down the street to my mothers' car.

"Mom?" Martin called out to me.

"Yes, son," I responded.

"Are you okay," he questioned.

"I'm fine."

I took a drag of my cigarette watching the strange people we surpassed. The rest of the way home was completely silent. In my current financial state, I won't be able to keep on going alone. There is no doubt in my mind that Sam's got some money stashed up somewhere. I just hope he didn't keep it in that busted ass car.

"I've got to hurry and get some gas, are you going to be okay, baby," my mother worried.

"Yeah, me and the boys will be just fine," I replied confidently.

We lazily got out of the car and Martin rushed around to my side opened the door and assisted me. Corey gave me an extensive hug, then helped me up to the porch. I turned back to wave a good bye to my mother, seated in the car, when I noticed a black truck just houses away. Slithering up the block toward us.

As Corey walked away to return to the car, the driver side window slowly came down and an arm rolled out. Before I could let out a shriek bullets tore from the vehicle aiming for my home.

Rodney dived to the ground yelling, "Get down!"

Martin and I plummeted to the gravel. Tires screeched as the car spun out to came back again, dumping shells from bullet casings onto the street. The black four door continued up the street out of our view. A calm fell over me before Martin shouted.

"Corey!"

I stayed on the floor, grinding my head into the pavement, "Please, please, please no."

Tears crowded Martin's eyes as he used his shirt to wipe the gushing blood from Corey's wide-open mouth. Rodney was on the phone with the police as my Mother scarcely got out of her car. I couldn't look up to see what was happening.

"Mom!" Martin called out to me.

"Stacy, Stacy!" my mother said in a panic rushing over to me.

She thought I had been shot, too. Rodney snatched me up from off the dirty ground. Though, I fell to my knees all over again. Across the yard from me, Martin sat on the ground with Corey, bloody and motionless rested in his arms.

"No!" I screamed to the top of my lungs, "God!"

Martin rapidly rocked forward and back with his head rested upon Corey's head, "Don't die, don't die...please don't die, brother!"

Corey chocked and gagged his eyes gaping wide.

## (Sirens)

The ambulance arrived within ten minutes, we gathered on the porch as they carefully placed Corey on the stretcher and rushed him off to hospital. My mother got in the ambulance with him. Martin whirled around went inside with Rodney trailing behind him. I took a drag of my cigarette tossed it over into the yard and returned inside. Martin startled me at the front door drenched in his brothers' blood. He stood ready with a loaded gun gripped tightly in his palm. Before anyone outside noticed, I slammed the front door shut.

"Martin," I said calmly, holding both hands out at my sides, "Baby, don't…please."

Tears flourished, my heart thudded faster as I barricaded the door from allowing Martin to pass. When I looked into my sons' eyes, I did not recognize him. I knew for sure that he would do something very wrong. Rodney rushed out of the room halfway dressed, in an effort to keep up with Martin. Martin stared me down as if I were the enemy, I watched as he sluggishly brought the gun up to his chin. Tears streamed down the sides of his face as he gestured to kill himself looking me dead in my eyes. Martin was dramatically shaking. I stood still and held my ground as he dropped to his knees and the gun fell with him. I cautiously drew nearer to Martin and held him close to my bosom. Stroking his head.

"It's okay baby…Corey will be okay."

"Why?" Martin uttered.

I peered over his shoulder into Rodney's eyes, then held my free arm open to hold him also. Tears soaking my shirt.

"He's going to be just fine."

# Hospital Hype

ast night I didn't sleep, I lay in my bed for hours staring into the darkness. Contemplating over Corey. Wondering what kind of needles, fidgets, and gadgets the doctors were poking and stabbing through him. The lobby seemed to be filled with mayhem. Across the room was a young boy, no older than six or seven, badly bruised with a questionable busted lip. He stared into my eyes staring back at him and he knew my heart hurt for him, such a sweet innocent little baby. Pressure weighed on me, I excused myself from his presence and went to ball my eyes out in the restroom. Then cleaned up before returning to the lobby. Once I opened the bathroom door Martin and Rodney stood before me with a man in a green jumper. I knew he had to have good news about Corey by the way he approached me with a near to happy smile.

"Mrs. Jacobs?" the doctor questioned.

"Yes, I'm she."

Whenever someone addressed me that way, I automatically assume it's going to be some bad, horrible, terrible news.

"Hi, I'm Dr. Gary Mallard," he shook my hand and quickly began to ruffle through the papers he possessed.

Martin angrily observed Dr. Mallard as if he weren't moving fast enough. Rodney stood on the other side of me squeezing my hand.

"We've done everything in our power, he's stabilizing very well, though were going to have to monitor his heart rate and breathing just to be sure his airway is not obstructed by any blood or excess saliva," he explained in great detail, "I'm sure he's going to pull through, your son is very strong."

After hearing that, I felt relieved though I don't want to see Corey like that. No mother wants to see her child passed out in the hospital. Chords and wires coiled around them with no conscious, or any recollection of what is taking place in their presence.

"He's in intensive care so I'm afraid there will be no visits right away, ma'am," he continued.

"When can we see him?" Martin interrupted.

Dr. Mallard paused and took notice of Martin's reaction.

"Soon, very soon I will see to it immediately," the doctor assured us, "But for now I will keep you updated of any changes and I do recommend going-."

"He'll live, right?" Martin interrupted again.

The doctor glared into his desperate eyes with compassion, amazed. Dr. Mallard positively responded to the question he almost wasn't confident in answering, "Yes, he'll live."

"Thank you, doctor," I said slowly letting go of Rodney's hand to throw my arm over Martin's shoulder, "Come on, baby."

We walked away distressed, my heartrending in anguish for my baby's happiness. I massaged Martin's shoulder as we retrieved to the car. The ride home was dead silent, we even rode without the radio playing. On the short ride, I thought about the black four door car and who could've been driving it. I also thought about how much more of the city's police department I was going to meet until they gave me my own badge. *Sigh* I wonder what Sam's thinking, I wonder what's going through his mind at this very moment.

Finally, we got home and on the porch was a familiar box. Similar, to the boxes my mother would get all the time when I was a kid. No bigger than a fourteen-inch television. I jumped out of the car and rummaged through my keys to get inside.

"Rodney, baby, grab that box," I requested.

There was an uncertainty in his response, though he hoisted the box inside. We each followed one after another into the kitchen to see what was left for us in the properly wrapped package.

"What is it?" Rodney asked, scratching his head, "It's got a little weight to it."

I examined the box for a mailing address, a name or anything on the outside to tell me more about what was on the inside. There was nothing.

"I'm not sure, but let's see."

Martin slit an opening along the top and ripped it open. Twenty-dollar bills flung out of the box. The three of us stood back from the table and each of us locked eyes with one another. We quarried through the box tossing bills in the air, fanning ourselves with money, then gained our morals back. We snatched up all the loose bills and rushed to my bedroom to properly count it out.

"I knew your daddy had something up his sleeve," I alleged.

"Damn, this is a lot of money," Martin responded, smiling for the first time in weeks.

"15, 1520, 1540, 1560, 1580, 16," Rodney went on and on beneath his breath rapidly snatching bills from hand to hand.

My boys and I accounted for twenty-thousand dollars inside of the hefty box. I counted out two-thousand right away and gave each of them a thousand. With the rest of the money, I planned on paying for Corey's hospital bill, whatever the insurance didn't cover anyway.

"How did Dad do this?" Martin wondered still counting.

"Your Dad knows magic tricks."

# In the Process of Expense

The police had positively identified the driver of the black four door car as Donny Wright, Omar's little brother. I guess he did just what the boys had done or was thinking about doing. If only his mother were there to stop him, he'd be walking around free and Corey would be alright. I'm still not sure of exactly where the money came from. Who better than Sam? I thought long and hard about it as I sat on the porch, in my favorite spot smoking my stresses away. The sun shinned brilliantly through faint clouds. Now that I'm not completely stressed out, I can enjoy the little things. The utility bills are paid up for about six months and I put a couple thousand down on the mortgage. The rest is for Corey's hospital bills and saving for the future. It's only been a couple weeks since Sam had been sentenced, I'm sure they'd allow him to call me. At least to tell me he's okay.

"Mom, it's Dad," Martin interrupted my thoughts, handing me the cordless phone.

"Hello."

"Stacy, baby?"

"Sam! I've been so worried about you we haven't heard anything and-"

"Stacy, Stacy, whoa, slow down I can't even understand you, calm down, look," he interrupted, "I'm in Pueblo, baby."

"Pueblo?" I asked puzzled, "PUEBLO?"

"Yeah, I'm sorry, Stacy," Sam said, "I don't mean to send you and the boys through this."

"We need you, Sam," I cried, "The house got shot up, Corey is in the hospital and I don't know how you did it, but we got it."

"Are you serious? Is he okay?" he babbled, "Got what? What are you talking about, Stacy?"

"The...the family sent us some gifts and I thought..."

"Wait, don't say too much," he stopped me.

We had twenty minutes to talk and I milked every second of it, just telling him how I felt and how much we all miss him. Though, our conversation went well it put me in more of a runt. If Sam doesn't know about the package, then who did it come from? Is this what my mother was getting in her boxes all those years ago? She would keep me home from school just to make sure her packages got inside. Before hanging up I allowed Martin to speak to his father.

"What did he say, son?"

"He said take all of our stuff and leave," Martin responded.

I sighed, "And, go where?"

# Shipping Out

Corey's gotten better, he's back with his Grandmother. Thank God that the bullets that ripped through her car didn't impale her, too. Regardless, she had to be checked out. Another package came this month and this time we weren't smiling. I came home from work to find the boys sitting at the kitchen table with the unopened box. As soon as I stepped foot into the kitchen I felt a blanket of anxiety sweep over me. I peered down at the familiar package that contained no labels or markings. Rodney and Martin peered at me unaware of what to do.

"Mom, where is this coming from?"

I placed my keys and purse on the counter, opened the package and rummaged through the box of money. It had to have been more because the box was filled to the top this time. I hopelessly looked into my sons' eyes looking back at me, desperate for an honest answer. An answer that I didn't have for him.

"It's not from your dad," I explained, "We need to go and talk to your, Grandma Terry."

"To Grandma Terry?" he questioned, "Why?"

Just before I could finish speaking there was an urgent knock at the door. The boys took the box back to my room and put it in the attic space with the rest of the money. I let them know to take out two-thousand dollars each and stay in the back room. I spied out the peep hole and was relieved to see that it was my mother on the other side. When I opened the door, she whooshed in right past me.

"Hey, mom, I was just about to call you I'm so glad you're here!" I exclaimed.

"Cut the shit, Stacy, you've been getting it for a month now," she spat.

My mother paced the floor then started down the hall way.

"Mom, wait," I pleaded gesturing her over to the kitchen table, "Sit down."

"Horse shit!" she began to weep, "I did everything for you and that man, and this is how he repays me?"

"Charles, my dad?" I questioned puzzled, "Daddy's doing this? But, that doesn't make sense how is he able to-,"

"It's not your damn money! So, it's none of your damn business, okay! Give me the packages," she demanded, "Now!"

I was floored. I had no idea that my dad was giving my mom money for all these years. Now, I know he loves me! She never showed any signs of having big money. Mom forgot I haven't been in her care since I had adopted my first child. Even when I did live with her, she wasn't being the mother she should've been. I don't understand why if we had the money. We could've been happy. What was she doing with the money?

"No."

"No? After everything that I've done for you, you got the nerve to tell me no?"

"What have you done for me besides have me?"

My mother snatched her neck, stepped back and placed a hand over her heart. Her jaw was literally on the floor.

"I took care of you!"

"You didn't even put food in the house! You slept with my husband! Now, you want some money from me?" I teased.

"Charles gave me that money!" She hollered.

"For me to have!" I corrected my Mother, "What were you doing with it anyways?"

Rodney and Martin stood in the hallway out of sight listening to my mother and I argue. Martin was shocked by what he was hearing. His Grandma slept with his Dad.

"That's my money and you know it's my money," my Mother cried, "I've got bills, I've got to pay your Grandma Sarah's bills and now I got your little boy! The one you decided to keep anyway."

I was in awe. How could she say something like that? She is right. There is no justification for giving him away now. I married the issue and had more children. I should've looked for him. Still, it doesn't give her any right to say anything about it to me. I pray to

God that my boys didn't hear her from the back room. I was stuck inside of my own thoughts momentarily just staring at the bad habit I called a mother. Out of complete anger I slapped her. Then, I slapped her again and pushed her towards the front door.

"Don't touch me!"

My mother lashed back at me just before I heard my son coming to save the day.

"Mom, stop it!" He scolded, "Don't hit my Grandma! What are you doing?"

"Get the hell out of my house."

"I'm going to get you, Stacy," she warned, "I'm going to get your ass good!"

Just before she turned to leave out the door she turned back to Martin and devilishly smiled.

"Your mom was a little whore," she spat before turning back to me, "She gave your brother away because she didn't love him."

I charged towards her just before Rodney grabbed me by the waist and held me back. My mother scarcely ran out of the house and slammed the door behind her. I wriggled out of Rodney's grip and went to Martin who was still standing in the same spot with a dumbstruck look upon his face. I stood before him and placed my hands on his shoulders.

"Son, please listen to me, I-," I started to explain.

"Is it true?" Martin interrogated.

Martin's eyes cut at me like a thousand blades. I could feel every pinch in my heart and it was nearly ready to explode.

"Son, please listen-."

"Tell me!" He screamed in my face, infuriated, "I have another brother?"

"Yes."

Unaware of what to do he trailed away from me and into the back room. Martin pulled a bag out and filled it with clothes. I followed behind him sobbing uncontrollably.

"I was fifteen years old I was just a kid," I protested, "I was scared, your dad was always kicking my ass when I was pregnant with him! I was scared for my baby! I was afraid he was going to kill us!"

"Liar!" Martin bellowed, "Why would you marry him then?"

"Because I love him! And I wasn't going to let my decision hurt my baby!" I informed him, "Sam changed."

Martin stood in awe unsure of what to believe. If I hadn't ever told him then I was just lying to him, through his eyes. He shook his head in disappointment at me down on my hands and knees in the middle of his bedroom. Tears pouring from my eyes like the rushing waters of Niagara Falls.

"So, where is he? Where is my brother?"

"Honey, I don't know I swear," I pleaded, "I should've been looking for him."

I put my head down in shame and seriously began to consider looking for my child at that very moment. Martin scoffed at me on the floor looking silly. He grabbed his bag and stepped right over me with no remorse.

"You're a liar!"

"Wait, bro," Rodney stopped him, "I'll come with you."

Martin paused momentarily and once again shook his head no.

"Nah, stay here," he responded.

"No."

Rodney stood grounded in amazement. I sat on the floor breathless Martin has never talked to me like that. Now, I knew for sure that my family was on the brink of collapse if it hadn't already.

"Where are you going?" I questioned, "Martin!"

Without responding, Martin waltzed out of the house and slammed the door shut behind him. Moments after the door slammed a huge rock crashed into my front window and shattered my glass coffee table. I rushed into the front room with Rodney following close behind only to find glass everywhere. Through the broken window, we could see Martin pick up his bag from the middle of the lawn and continue on his way down the street. I fell to my knees and burst into prayer.

"Father God, please help me in this dark time," I prayed with my head to the ceiling.

Rodney stood silent behind me glaring at the back of my head.

"Ms. Stacy...Ms. Stacy are you okay?"

"I'm fine, son," I replied, "I'll be just fine."

I got up and went to the basement looking for old boxes and duct tape to patch up my front window. Rodney had already begun sweeping up the glass.

"Thank you, son," I said graciously.

For a moment, I paused and reflected on Rodney. 'My, son,' I thought to myself. It could be him but, what are the odds of my baby finding his way back to me. It's just too much of a coincidence. Besides, I'm sure I would feel something I'm sure my motherly instinct would have kicked in by now. I'm sure he would've felt something more than me. Damn, the thought of it just totally and completely disgusts me. If Rodney is my child I gave him away like he was nothing. Aside of that, I had three more children and never looked back.

After picking up the glass, I retired to my bedroom. It was dark, lonely and I longed for Sam to be here with me. If I could just get a call from him at this very moment it would make me feel better. I'm at my wits end and ready to get away. A warm shower and a comfortable bed called for me. I spread out across the mattress and turned to some comedy on the television set. My mind was filled with images of my son walking in the dark, cold streets. I could picture him walking up to the front door and into my bedroom to apologize to me. To tell me that he loved me and that he would never disrespect me again. I've got to get my babies home before something else goes wrong that could have been prevented. If only I had known how life would turn out. I would've kept my child with me and Sam, I would've never let him go. I didn't want the baby to have anything to do with Sam. I thought that Sam would leave me alone for good and I would have my life back. Hopeful, that my baby would have a better life. I would have tried to finish school.

Faint footsteps ascended toward the door, then finally an unsure knock. I lazily rose to my feet, opened the door and welcomed Rodney in. He stood in the middle of the room until I sat down, then he plopped down next to me with a reluctant smile.

"You feel better," Rodney curiously questioned.

"Do I ever," I joked just before falling apart, "I don't want you to see me like this, son."

"I appreciate you for letting me stay here," he began, "But, I'm going to go now I feel like a lot of this is my fault…thank you all for never blaming me."

"No, wait please," I begged, "I can't stay here by myself tonight, not until that window gets fixed."

Panic consumed me. It was already after dark outside and strange people are always walking around my neighborhood. There is traffic all through the night in the alley behind my house, sometimes at three and four o'clock in the morning. If Rodney left tonight I'd have one more stressful thing on my plate and no one here to help protect the house. I'd have to stay up all night with the gun. I cried hysterically as I begged him not to go.

"This is my fault," I confessed, "I should have been better."

"Don't say that," Rodney disagreed, "I'll stay."

He held me in his arms and cradled me like a baby just like Sam used to. Gently swaying back and forth.

"I'm going to put you in the bed, Mom," he whispered, "So you can be comfortable, okay."

"Okay."

Rodney took a deep breath and kissed my forehead before gracefully rising to his feet. He helped me to get under the sheets then tucked me in. Strange, it made me feel so safe and so loved. I hope someone tucked my son in every night, wherever he is.

"I'm going to go in the front room," Rodney informed me, "Get some rest, Mom."

"Goodnight, son."

Thank God, I can honestly say I'm glad that Rodney is here with us. Now that Sam won't be coming home any time soon. I need my babies and we need Father Gods love now more than ever. Rodney escaped into the darkness to the front room. He cuddled into the couch cushions and popped on the television. Just as I did, he prayed before bed. God will protect them, God will protect all of us. I'm starting to love Rodney just like he is one of my boys. His appearance shows those strong Native traits, just like my mother. If it was true, then I didn't want him because I gave him away. I silently wept to myself until I fell fast asleep.

In the silence of the night, Martin came crashing through the front door. Rodney quickly rose up and went for his gun under the cushion before realizing who it was. Rodney stood to his feet concerned and rushed over to the door.

"What's wrong, bro? What happened?" He pried.

"Mom! Mom!" Martin screamed, "Where's she at?"

Over hearing the commotion, I leaped out of bed and dashed into the front room terrified. Though, I was happy to see Martin home safely he was completely out of breath and missing his bag.

"What's going on, son," I said seating myself on the loveseat, "Are you okay? Where's your bag?"

"Somebody is following me," Martin blurted out, "Two dudes in a grey truck been following me all night!"

"What?" I questioned frantically, "Did you see their faces?"

"Not really, no, I just ran!"

"Where did this happen at? Where were you, son?"

Martin took a deep breath while pacing around the family room.

"I first saw them when I left the house earlier at the end of the block and then I saw the same car, same dudes again when I was leaving, Reggie's house." Martin stated, breathing heavily, "When I ran they started driving after me!"

Each of my boys gathered with me as I squeezed them tight. I need Sam, if he were here this would not be happening. I'm sure of it. In my mind I prayed repeatedly for my babies. Including, Corey and Sam, I can't believe my family is being ripped apart like this.

"Go pack some of your things," I whispered to them, "Hurry."

"I'm sorry."

"It's okay, Martin, I know," I hugged my baby boy, then scooted him away, "Hurry, please, we've got to get out of here, now."

We ran around the house like it was ten second clean up time grabbing everything that we could sustain. Martin made especially sure to grab my gun with all the money. We quickly dashed out the back door to the garage, got into my vehicle and raced down the alley.

There was a beautiful hotel on the way out to the airport. All I could think was maybe my mother did this, the entire ride. I don't put anything past anyone. Not murder past Sam or Corey. My mother doesn't have a heart, although she hates pain. Just as much as she hates seeing someone else going through it. She had to of asked someone, or ones for that matter, to do this for her. My son did say that there were two men coming for him. It dawned on me. We have the damn money! So, maybe the same two men Detective Moss showed me a picture of are the same two men trying to do Lord knows what to my son. Maybe it's their money, but then how did I get it. If it's truly coming from my Dad, maybe he knew about my family. Maybe Mom told him, but then again maybe not. Dad never wrote to me anyways.

# Clarity

My cell bounced around immensely throughout the morning.

"Mom," Martin spoke, "Please get your phone."

My arm stretched out of the thick warm blankets and snatched my cell from the dresser. I propped up my head and glared over at my boys comfortably rested. Rodney sprawled out in the bed, and Martin on the couch close by.

"Hello," I grumbled.

"Mom!" Corey yelled through the phone, "Just listen to me, okay, I want you guys to pack all your stuff and come get in the truck, now! Don't say anything else just get up and let's go, now!"

"Corey," Slowly, my body lifted from the fluffed pillows, "Where are you?"

"In the parking garage," he informed me, "Next to your car."

"How did y-"

Corey shouted, "Mom! I'll explain in the car, hurry!"

"Okay, okay, okay," I panted.

I hurried out of bed to wake Rodney and Martin then quickly packed what little we had. I wondered what could be happening now. Sam had to of called by now he knows the number to my cell. It's been so long since I've talked to him I'm starting to feel like he doesn't love me as much as I do him. He doesn't love us. Don't get me wrong, he's changed for the best, but I've always felt this way about Sam. I mean, why is any of this happening? I literally do not have a clue. I feel like an idiot. I glanced over at Martin and Rodney throwing their things together for just a second. I could see the fear in their eyes, I could feel it piercing my heart.

From the room to the parking lot to get to the vehicles, I cried. I wonder who Corey could have come with. Unless my mother has been doing him some kind of good. She seems to be changing as well.

"Where's he at, Mom?" Martin questioned.

"I'm not sure, son," I said scoping the parking lot, "He said by our car."

We began to load our bags into the car as a grey truck pulled up behind us, blocking me in. From the corner of my eye, I could hear and see Martin's immediate reaction.

"That's the truck!" He shouted in amazement.

Corey quickly got out the car and reassured us that it was safe to get inside and to leave my vehicle.

Rodney and Martin were armed and ready for anything to go wrong. I've never felt so unsure in my life, still I held onto the duffle bag tight. As we packed into the back the driver stared me directly in my eyes with a slightly warm smile stretched across his face. It was him! The man from the photo Detective Moss showed to me. I recognize his deep, dark brown eyes that literally pull you right in and again a red hue to his light skin. Just like me! The man in the passenger's seat swiveled his large body around to greet me with a smile. He too was the man pictured in the other photograph. His bald head glistened with beads of visible sweat in the sun. They are the people, these are the money launderers and I think we have their money, I think. This is crazy yet for some reason I'm no longer afraid. They feel so familiar, like I know these men. Obviously, they know exactly who I am.

"Wow, Stacy," the driver let out with an awkward sigh, "You're all grown up."

As if I was stuck in the twilight zone, I peeked over at Corey glaring back at me with a slight smile. This must be a blessing. I haven't seen my baby smile in a long time, since before Chane died. I peered over my shoulder into the back row of seats at Rodney and then toward Martin on the other side. He had his eyes fixated on the strange men. I reached back and placed my hand on his knee then tapped him to grab his attention.

"We didn't mean to scare you little man," the passenger stated, "Looked to me like you needed some help."

"Who are you?" He asked angrily.

"Yo, man, don't be rude," Corey told him.

"It's alright, nephew," the driver responded respectful of Martin's reaction, "I'm your uncle, Lonnie, and this here my younger brother, Ricky,"

"We're your dad's little brothers, Stacy, I know you probably don't remember us," Ricky explained, "But, we were there for you and your Mom a while back."

"Where's my Grandpa?" Martin questioned excitedly.

"He's locked up young buck," Lonnie responded with a sigh.

Ricky exhaled, "Yeah, we haven't seen your Grandfather in a long time."

"How did you know where we were," I asked concerned looking to Corey for answers.

"That's not important," Corey told me, "We have to go...there is nothing left for us here."

I hung my head low then quickly looked back at Corey, "There's something I have to tell you, son, you have a-."

"Another brother," Corey said without a break, "I know."

"Grandma told you, huh?"

He noticeably shook his head no, "Dad told me and Chane a long time ago, but he told us never to say anything about it."

I held my head up toward the roof of Lonnie's truck and shut my eyes together tight. I once again found myself praying to God, hoping that this is all just a dream. My heart is so full of sorrow, regret, and for the first time in a long time, literal hatred. I hate my life right now. I could feel Rodney's strong hand message my shoulder from the back seat as I squeezed Corey's hand tight.

"Grandma left early this morning then my uncles showed up and told me to pack my things and get in the truck with them," he informed me, "I didn't know what else to do, Mom and I'm not going to lie...I was afraid."

"Your dad left you a house...it's in Ken Caryl," Lonnie interrupted, "You do what you want with it, but I advise you live there for now until Terry calms down."

Ricky wiped the sweat on his head with a towel.

"Yeah, she's so damn mad she done tore up her house and yours," Ricky accidentally told me.

"My house?" I said in a panic as I began to pout, "What's wrong with my house?"

Lonnie angrily glanced over at Ricky then explained, "You and the boys weren't there, that's most important."

"What?" I grew anxious, questioning my uncle, "What do you mean by that?"

"I'll show you."

Corey let out a deep sigh of frustration. My eyes locked onto Corey he knows more about what's going on than any of us. When we pulled onto our street, I shut my eyes and didn't open them to face the horror until I heard Corey say, "Look, mom."

Reluctant, I opened my eyes to find nothing there. My house was literally a pile of rubble. Thank God Martin came home when he had, or Rodney and I would probably be rubble, too. People stood around looking on in shock. Vehicles passing by slowed to a complete stop just to see the breath-taking vision.

"She did this?" I questioned.

"Yeah," Lonnie confessed, "Your dad couldn't

wait until you were old enough, your mama wasn't doing right, and she didn't want us to find you."

"Get me out of here," I begged, slumping down in the seat.

We drove past my mothers' half burned down house and watched as the on lookers crowded her lawn, too. It was like all the bad memories burned up with the house. She'd probably be able to recover some of her things. The front room of our house was completely gone. Along with our family photos. The kitchen sink and the fridge were barely noticeable in the rubble. All that was left was the back of the house where our bedrooms once existed.

"Damn, what are we going to do now? Where is she now?" I frantically questioned.

"We're going to survive, mama," Corey reassured me.

What's gotten into him? Maybe he had an epiphany. Corey nearly died. My son held me close under his arm with his warm cheek rested on top of my head. My tears soaked through his shirt as I watched my childhood home disappear off into the distance. Sam is never going to believe half of the things I have to tell him. I wish he was here with me now; I need him more than ever.

# Westbound

The drive was a little over an hour long and I began to doubt if I wanted to live so far away from Denver. It's not like I have friends or anything, thanks to Sam. As well as, the only family that I truly have that love and care for me are all right here with me in the truck. I rested my head on Corey's shoulder. The murder was the furthest thing from my mind. I was so happy to see my baby I didn't even think about it. We peered out of the windows and watched in amazement as the mountains grew larger than life. I could feel a literal change in the atmosphere. Every now and then I had to yawn to rid my ears of pressure building up from the elevation. The view was so beautiful and a little frightening at the same time. We slipped between two large mountains and into a luscious, green valley. I was truly taken by rolling hills covered in pine trees and red rocks that seemed to stalk the land. Everywhere I looked I seen proof that there is an almighty God. The closer we got to the neighborhood the more and more I wanted to stay here forever. It was like a little slice of heaven.

"Here we are," Lonnie said excitedly.

We arrived in front of a beautiful two-story home. From the outside, I was looking at a three-car garage mansion. Tan in color with a white trim and a big beautiful porch made of wood that was also painted white. We galloped up the stairs to the solid, light wooden door covered in beautiful stained glass for windows. Lonnie had fallen behind the crowd attempting to take my house key from his key ring. He came up the stairs directly to me and handed off the key.

"Welcome home," Lonnie told me, "Only you have a key here, you and the boys are safe here."

"I can't wait to see what the inside looks like," Martin expressed.

Rodney stumble up the stairs in shock, "Wow."

"Open the door, Mom," Corey urged.

I took a deep breath and smiled before turning the key and twisting the knob. As soon as I stepped inside my attention was immediately captured by the double stair case that lead up to a long and wide-open hallway. Rodney and Martin dashed up either side of the stair case at top speed and down the long hall to explore. Lonnie and Ricky walked all about the house with me and Corey. I have so many questions for them I want to know so much about them, but I need to know the most important thing now.

"How did you find us?" I questioned, following close behind, "How did you know where we were?"

Lonnie paused and turned to me with his hands held together, "Don't freak out like nephew did, but I followed you...we knew where you all were all week long."

"I don't know what to say."

The high ceilings made me feel so small. I slowly inched toward Corey, grabbed for my sons' hand and squeezed it in fear.

"We don't know who you are," I continued in tears.

"Mom," Corey held on to me tight, "Look at them...they look just like us."

Every ounce of fear left my body and the sweetest calm fell upon me. When I looked into my sons' eyes then back to the so called "strangers" that stood before me. I could see it, too. I could see them in my son. Mostly Lonnie, his leadership over Ricky reminded me of Chane. I threw my hands over my face in shame and fell to my knees. I have no idea what to do with myself at this point.

"Don't let Martin see me," I begged.

"It's okay, momma," Corey joined me down on the plush carpet, "It's a lot to take in."

"Excuse me," I said with my face to the floor, "I can't take this right now...I'm sorry."

Ricky turned away and sulked to himself. Lonnie held back his tears and took a knee on the other side of me. Lonnie took in a breath, as he gently rubbed my back.

"Stacy, we're here for you now, okay."

Corey glared over his shoulder at Ricky still facing

the corner, sulking. He turned back to Lonnie and seen that he had also began to cry. Corey brought his attention back to me on the floor beside him in pieces. Suddenly, the pain that he felt for us grew stronger.

Ricky whipped around and blurted, "We were there for you, Stacy and we love you!"

"Yeah," Lonnie said with a sigh, "We were there… you were too little to remember, but we were there."

"Things happened, baby girl," Ricky said hysterically, "Your daddy…we all had to do some time, but we sent that money!"

Before long we were all in the middle of the main floor hallway in tears. I could hear Martin and Rodney still running about. Mentally, I knew I had to hurry and get myself together. I quickly rose to my feet and dusted my clothes off.

"I'm sorry," I told Corey, "I don't want you to see me like this."

"It's okay," my son replied hugging me tight, "You're okay, momma."

I let out one more cry as I squeezed Corey back. Before I said another word, I brushed my hair back with my fingers.

"Nobody knew your mama wasn't giving you no money," Lonnie explained, "Until your Grandma Sarah finally told us."

"She ain't no better than your, Mom," Ricky pointed out, "She got some of that money, too, and didn't even tell us until you went and stayed there. I called her from jail and she told all on your, momma."

I continuously wiped tears away from my eyes, "So, you know about her and their dad, too?"

"What?" My uncles questioned in unison.

"No, nothing," I replied waving them off, "I'm going to get some sleep, okay, I-."

"Wait, there's one last thing we're going to show you, Stacy before we leave," Ricky reminded his brother.

"Oh yes! You're going to need another key for this, niece," Lonnie said wiping the tears from his face.

Can't this little tour end until another day, I'm so tired. Still, Corey and I followed them down into the basement level of the house. When the lights popped on I was completely amazed! I almost forgot that I was just ready for bed a second ago. The basement is enormous, it's like our own personal bar area. The walls are made completely of mirrors and the floor isn't carpeted. Instead, there is a smooth black cement the same texture as the bar. With golden shelves and more mirrors. All the bottles that filled the many shelves seemed to be untouched. I peeked over to look at Corey's expression. He had already left my side to fix himself a stiff drink. I chuckled to myself then proceeded to follow Lonnie and Ricky into a space behind the bar. Do to the fun house effect I couldn't see that the bar was hiding a corridor. Only a closer examination under a bright light would reveal a key hole that didn't require a knob. Simply unlock the door and push it open. Pretty stealth if you ask me.

"Here," Ricky said with a smile handing off another key, excited to show me what was inside.

I nervously unlocked the door and we each piled into the room. When I turned on the light all I could see were packages littered all over the place. Packages just like the ones my mom would get when I was a kid. Just like the two packages that came to my front door. I rapidly turned to Lonnie and gave him a big hug and Ricky as well because I was so enamored. They were full of money.

"I know you know what this is!" Lonnie exclaimed.

"Each of these boxes has twenty or forty large inside," Ricky explained, "Your daddy saved this money for you, Stacy so you didn't have to work again a day in your life."

"Your daddy loves you, Stacy," Lonnie continued, "He's going to give you a call. I let him know when he called yesterday that Terry was acting up and you were going to need this place now more than ever."

"Why didn't he call before? He never wrote to us or anything?" I questioned, teary eyed.

"Why don't you ask him yourself?" Ricky suggested, "Get you some rest, niece, we're going to get out of here."

"When will you come back, I mean, I've only just gotten to know you we can have a few drinks if you'd like," I coaxed.

"Trust me, we'll be back to get to know you guys better," Lonnie replied placing a hand on my shoulder, "There is nothing else we'd rather do, but we got to take care of business first."

"We'll take you all to meet some other members of the family soon," Ricky proposed.

Corey and I followed behind them as we gathered up the stairs and to the front door to say our farewells. Rodney and Martin had come down just in time before Lonnie and Ricky had gone.

"It's nice to meet you guys," Martin expressed, thankful.

"You'll be seeing a lot more of us young buck," Lonnie said just before locking eyes on Rodney, "Is this your friend here?"

"That's my brother's keeper," Corey spoke up.

"I'm Rodney, sir," he said for himself.

"Rodney, huh, I respect you…nephew," Ricky told him, with a solid fist over his heart.

"I'm sorry we couldn't stay long, but we'll be around," Lonnie said, "Sorry, we scared you little man."

"It's cool," Martin replied shrugging him off.

"There is fresh food in the kitchen and if the boys smoke a little ganja you'll find some beneath the bar," Ricky added, "Don't tell, Sarah where you all are at."

"Nobody says anything," Lonnie scolded, cutting his eye at each of us, "Just chill."

Suddenly, I felt uncomfortable and overwhelmed again. I couldn't wait to say my goodbyes, wave them off and shut the damn door. We all watched from the porch as they raced down the street. The boys and I raced inside to choose our rooms and settle in. We didn't need a car anymore and the entire house was already fully furnished. I quickly got out of my dingy clothes and happily slid into my glass shower. I got out covered myself with a plush body towel and explored my suite. All we were missing was Sam and Chane. As much as I anticipated on talking to my father, Charles, I want to talk to Sam even more so. To let him know what's going on and where we are. He's probably called the house by now, I'm sure of it. I wonder what he's doing at this very minute, I know that he's thinking of me. I wonder if he's warm, comfortable or being properly fed. Hopefully he isn't in any kind of trouble down there in Pueblo.

My thoughts were immediately interrupted by a knock on my bedroom double doors. I bundled up in a silk robe that I assumed to be mine then went to the doors and flung them both open. Rodney, Corey and Martin stood in amazement shocked by how large my room is. They especially loved my California king sized canopy bed draped in pearl white satin.

"Damn, Mom!" Martin said shoving past me, "You have a huge room! This is bigger than our kitchen and our front room were combined!"

"Nice, it's a princess bed," Rodney pointed out.

"You guys want to watch a movie?" I asked walking towards the television, "It'll take our minds off of this crazy damn day."

"Mmm," Corey began with doubt, "Maybe later."

I stopped dead in my tracks then spun back around to give them my undivided attention. Now, I'm starting to think that there is something wrong. I can't take any more blows. My boys stood in the middle of the room as they each stole a glance at one another then looked to me. I was just dying to know what they were about to say. The anxious expressions on their faces pushed me to assume that they didn't have any good news for me.

"What's going on?" I asked frantically.

"We were going to go and have a smoke, Mom," Martin replied, "Come down and talk with us."

I asked no more questions and followed behind them into our new luxurious basement. The boys watched as I whisked past them to the room behind the secret wall and brought out one of the packages. My boys were each seated at a stool in the bar area where I placed the package between us. Since we were having a talk I figured it was the best time of any to tell them about the same packages my mother, their Grandma Terry, would receive.

"You know," I began as I tore the package open, "My mama would keep me home from school to bring these packages in the house...I never knew what was in them."

"Really, just like these?" Rodney questioned.

"Yup, before I went to live with Grandma Sarah," I continued, "I would've never guessed it was money."

I paused, placed my hands on the bar top and dropped my head. Before I completely fell to pieces in front of my boys, I felt Corey grasp my hand. Tears rained from my eyes as I threw my head to the ceiling and squeezed his hand back. I brought my attention back to the package attempting to overcome the emotions.

"It's okay, Momma, don't cry," Corey pleaded.

"Your right, son...and that's why," I continued, pulling stacks of money from the box, "I give it to you...my babies. Before we go upstairs I want each of you to take a package into your room, it'll be yours."

"Mom, we know you love us," Martin assured me, "You don't have to do this."

"He's right, Momma, we don't need that money," Corey responded.

Rodney sat between the two of them and slouched over on the bar with his head rested on his arms glaring through the mirror top. I placed a large stack of crisp one-hundred-dollar bills in front of Corey.

"I didn't get a chance to give you what I gave them, baby," I replied, turning my attention to Rodney, "You okay, son, you haven't said much today?"

He sat at attention and took a deep breath, "I'm okay."

Corey sat the money back on the bar and leaned in toward me.

"That's what we wanted to talk about, Mom," Corey started.

"I think this is my brother!" Martin blurted out, "Rodney's our older brother."

I quickly whipped around to the golden shelves behind me and searched frantically for anything dark and rich with honey. I snatched a bottle down, cracked it open and drank away. My face shriveled up as I swallowed the burning liquor. I was so fucking disgusted with myself. I should have never given my baby away. If I thought the same, that for one moment he was my son, too. What exactly does that make me look like? On the inside I was panicking as I slowly built up the urge to turn around and face my boys. The tears in my eyes clouded my vision and when I finally faced each of them I could see it. I could see that in of each their eyes there was the same burning desire to be brothers. In each of their hazel eyes that looked just like mine, and their brown skin tinted red just like me. Rodney's jet, black braids streamed down to the middle of his back like my mothers' beautiful hair. I could see the resemblance in each of their high cheek bones and the muscles that clinched in each of their strong jaws. The expensive bottle slowly fell from my grasp and I collapsed to the ground with it.

"Mom!" Corey quickly reacted.

My muscle-bound son picked up my motionless body and carried me up two flights of stairs to my glorious bed. Martin and Rodney watched from my doorway as I came back to reality and cried to Corey.

"Just get some sleep, Mom," Corey tried convincing me.

"No, baby please let me say this."

He sat at the edge of my plush mattress and glared into my eyes anticipating on what I had to say. I slowly sat up and searched for my other two boys.

"Martin! Rodney!" I called out, still shaken, "Get in here!"

They each rushed to my bedside along with Corey. I swayed from side to side dividing my attention up amongst them. I peered into one set of teary eyes, then another and another.

"Rodney," I started, "Do you believe I'm your Mom?"

Rodney looked to the ground for answers, he does that whenever he's nervous. I know he felt just as funny about all this as I did.

"After, Ms. Terry said that you...you gave the baby away...I thought about it," he responded with his head down.

Even though Rodney and I talked about it before. He didn't tell me the truth about the way he felt.

"When did you give up our brother?" Corey interrogated.

"Before you and Chane were born...he would have been just a year older."

Corey looked over his shoulder to Rodney and Martin as if they knew the answer all along.

"Mom, Rodney is a year older than me and

Chane," Corey told me, "I'm telling you this is our brother."

I rested my head back on my pillows and gazed at the ceiling.

"We'll get a blood test," I started, "As soon as possible, as soon as my uncles come back to get us we'll go."

"Do you believe it?" Martin said, "Do you think he's our brother?"

Still looking to the ceiling, I noticeably shook my head, "I don't know, son."

"Well, I don't think we need a test," Corey said with confidence, "Tell her."

"I believe you're her," Rodney sighed and locked eyes with me, "My mother."

My eyes burned from the tears. Rodney gazed into my face nodding his head yes.

"We fought a lot, Mom," Martin added, "Like brothers."

"He's got our eyes, our skin, our-,"

"Our hearts...and, our love," I interrupted, Corey, "...It could be."

Martin shouted, "It is him!"

I shamefully wiped the tears from my face and sighed. I didn't know what to say to my boys. I knew I wasn't going to allow them to believe in something that I didn't know to be absolutely true.

"I'm not going to lie...I want the blood test so we can be absolutely sure," I expressed.

Corey threw an arm around Rodney and Martin then looked to me with pride.

"Chane told me," he stated, "In my dream he said it to me, Mom...we don't need a blood test."

The boys filed out one by one and left me alone, afraid in my big quiet room. All I could think of was Chane. I cried hysterically because although I missed him dearly I wouldn't know what to do if he showed up in my dreams. I'm starting to think that Corey may actually be going crazy. Either that or he wants his brother back so bad that he's willing to use Rodney to fill the void. On top of that, Sam not being here is starting to take a toll on all of us. I turned on the television set, left my bedroom light on and even turned on the light in my luxurious bathroom. I prayed before bed and thanked God for protecting us. I even asked that he watch over my mother wherever she was.

Oh,

My love

Sweet love

I miss you so much I can't even sleep.
Every night that I lay in my bed, I
turn on my side and I weep.
Some nights I stare up at the sky and
wonder if you're thinking of me.
Other times I just lay there, and I
wish that your ass was free.
I even pray that I could kiss you and
just hold you in my hands.
But, then I cry and wonder why, you
just didn't give a damn?

# Family Talk

"**M**om, wake up," Corey called out softly shaking my shoulder, "Get up, Mom."

I rubbed my eyes and came to realization, "Yes, son."

"Wake up, Stacy," Lonnie joined in, "There's someone on the phone for you."

I rested all my weight on my elbow as I glared around the room at my family. I didn't think of who it could be or even why? I just wanted it to be Sam, but it couldn't be that, my uncles don't know him. I quickly gathered my thoughts then grabbed a hold of the phone and the receiver.

"Hello," I said nervously awaiting a response, jerking the tangled phone cord around.

"Baby girl," my father's deep, raspy voice exclaimed, "Hey!"

Everything in me went numb and words refused to come out of my parted lips. Silent tears began to stream down my face. I pray to God this isn't a dream.

"Daddy?" I cried out to him, "It's you?"

My face crinkled up like a raisin. Lumps filled my throat as I cried, gasping for air.

"Don't cry baby," he said sulking with me, "Daddy loves you, Stacy."

"Dad!" I shouted, and repeatedly called to him in disbelief, "Dad, dad, dad."

I have no words, all I can do is cry hysterically. Every word that comes out of his mouth shocks me. I hate that I can't hug him or look him in his face and tell him how much I love him. I hate that I don't even know him. I held the phone close to my chest as I sobbed in grief and reluctantly put it back to my ear.

"Why? Why? Why?" I pleaded.

"Daddy can't-"

Charles paused. He was hurting as much as I was. I could hear him on the other end choking up trying to hold back the tears. I'm thirty years old and I want my Dad.

"Daddy can't tell you why, baby girl."

Corey and Martin climbed into the bed with me as Rodney sat at the foot. I held out an arm to pull each of my boys in closer to me as tears flowed from my eyes.

"I love you, daddy," I expressed, "I never forgot about you."

"I love you, too and I thought about you every day don't let your Mama, your Grandma or nobody else tell you different," He assured me, "Every damn day!"

"Please, write me," I begged, "I want to talk to you...I have a family now and-"

"I didn't know what to write," My Dad cut in, "It was going to hurt daddy too bad to get a letter from you...you're older now and it still hurts."

"Wait, please, how can I write you?" I questioned, sulking.

"I know the address I'm going to write you and the kids, where they at?" he asked, "We don't have a lot of time, baby girl."

"Say hello to your Grandfather," I told the boys, holding the phone out toward them.

"What's up Grandpa," Corey blurted out.

"Hey, Grandpa," Martin added.

All eyes in the room rested on Rodney, we thought he wasn't going to say anything. He still feels like he's an outsider. Though, Corey and Martin quietly bullied a response out of him.

"Hi, Grandpa," Rodney said shyly.

"My boys!" he exclaimed "I'm Grandpa Charles, I'm going to write to you and send some pictures."

"He said he's going to send you guys some photos and letters."

"Okay!" they responded in unison.

Ricky and Lonnie stood aside and happily waited for us to finish talking to my father.

"Stacy," My father said in a serious tone, "Everything is going to be okay now...I didn't know your Mama wasn't taking care of you."

"I think she's trying to find us," I continued to cry, "And, I don't know what to do."

"She won't find you," My father, Charles, said to me, "I'm making sure of that, okay."

"I'm married," I tried talking through the tears, "his name is, Sam-

"I should've been there with you every day," he interrupted and continued to cry with me, "Daddy made some big mistakes."

"I don't care," I said honestly, "I just want to keep talking to you...I want to know who you are, I want you to know who we are."

My boys held back their tears as best as they could, but lately we've all been emotional and completely stressed out. Although, I thank God that we're together. I only wish that Sam could be here with us, too.

"I'm in Pueblo, baby...I know your man, I know your husb-"

"Sam!" I interrupted, "You're with my Sammy?"

"Dad!" Martin exclaimed, "Grandpa knows Dad?"

Confused, Corey glanced over his shoulder at Ricky and Lonnie both smiling back at him.

"How is he doing, Dad?"

"Don't worry about him," my Dad said, "He's doing just fine."

As if my Dad had already known who Sam was. If he has, I'm sure he realizes how long it's been since we've talked to Sam. I'm pretty sure Dad would have said something so that we could talk to Sam, too. Why wouldn't my Uncles tell me? Corey turned back to Rodney and Martin with a devilish smile then continued to listen in.

"He's, he's here," Charles stuttered with a chuckle, "I've been getting to know him better."

I planted my head in my palm and nodded as if he

could see me, "Please, tell him where we are, I haven't talked to him. Sam doesn't know where we are."

"He's going to call you real soon, baby girl," my father, Charles reassured me, "Just enjoy your new house, okay."

Tears poured from my eyes endlessly, "We will… thank you so much…I love you, Daddy."

Charles paused then cleared his throat before responding, "I love you, too…my little girl. Daddy's proud of you, okay."

There is a God. I hate that Sam hasn't been calling and checking on us for himself, though I'm glad to know where he is finally and hopefully he is okay.

"Let me talk to Lonnie, hurry," he demanded, "I don't have a lot of time, but I'll write you baby girl, I will."

Without another word I handed off the phone and covered my face completely with my hands. Lonnie quickly grabbed the phone then retreated out the door and down the hall. My head is so full of thoughts I'm beginning to crave shots of liquor. I was happy, angry, sad and confused all in one big bundle of sorrow and dread. Though, I must stay strong for my boys. Especially now that their facing a big battle too, thanks to me.

After a few seconds, I lifted my head to smile at my boys then took a deep breath to calm myself. Things truly are starting to get better.

"Martin, son, can you go get me the tray from beneath the bar, please?" I asked with a smile.

He leaped into action as Ricky sat in the plush loveseat on the other side of the room glaring at us all sincerely broken hearted. We've lost it all, yet somehow God is giving us so much more back. We're truly blessed.

"Rodney," I began as I reached for him taking a hold of his hand, "Son, can you go get a nice bottle of wine and glasses for us to celebrate."

Rodney smiled back at me as the heaviness of the room started to lift. The frowns on each of our faces grew to smiles. Corey lovingly patted Rodney on the back as he quickly got up to do as I asked. I could see Ricky's reaction begin to change from across the way. He stood to his feet walked over to the bed watching for Rodney to disappear down the hall. Just as he left Ricky locked eyes with me.

"Adopted?" he questioned sarcastically.

Before Corey could snap back I quickly said, "He's my son."

"He looks just like the boys," Ricky admitted, "But, I thought you said he was their..."

"My brother's keeper," Corey interrupted.

Ricky turned his attention to Corey and snatched his neck back in amazement, "Why not you, young blood? He was you."

In my opinion, Corey was starting to get angry and my uncle Ricky felt like he was being disrespected. Until now, I never thought anything of it myself, but I wonder the same thing. Maybe it was Corey's way of making Rodney feel more accepted or maybe he was filling in the gap. I looked on to my son and awaited his answer. Before Corey could say a word, Martin and Rodney each returned to the room with Lonnie following close behind.

"We didn't know which one you wanted, Mom," Rodney started, happily holding two big bottles of wine "So, I just grabbed some Merlot and some Moscato."

"Come on, Rick," Lonnie coaxed, "We got to head out, now."

Martin took his place beside Corey. Right away, he could see in Corey's expression that something was wrong. Rodney inched over to his seat at the edge of my big bed and watched as Corey nervously brushed his faded hair forward with his hand. Ricky started out the door as Lonnie waved his goodbyes.

"We'll see you all soon," Lonnie assured us.

Ricky turned back just before crossing the threshold, "That's real, nephew."

Lonnie looked on confused. Unfazed, they each rushed down the hall and out the door. I didn't want to say anything to set my son off, so I just reached over and rubbed his back. Corey pounded his fist against his knee and quickly stood to his feet.

"Give me a bottle," he demanded of Rodney

Reluctant, Rodney handed over the Merlot and a bottle opener. Corey snatched the bottle, popped the top off tossed the opener back on my bed and started for the door. Before he could leave, Martin rushed in front of him and closed both doors. He leaned his slender body up against them and locked the doors behind his back.

"Sit down, Corey," Martin yelled.

"Martin," Corey murmured with his head hung low.

"No!" Martin screamed louder, "Sit down, now!"

Rodney and I watched from my bed as my brave little boy stood up to his big brother. I was just praying Corey didn't take it the wrong way. Instead, he took a couple steps back and a swig of liquor straight from the bottle.

"Move, Martin," he begged, "I want to go talk to, Chane."

Chills ran up my spine as goose bumps covered my body from head to toe. I got so damn scared I choked up and could barely breathe for a few seconds. Rodney held his head down and glued his eyes to the carpet. I continued to look on in amazement as Martin scrambled for what to say to Corey.

"He's gone, he's not really there," Martin cried, "Stop saying that."

"Where is he, Corey?" I cut in out of curiosity, "Where do you see Chane?"

I got out of bed and rushed over to my crazy child. Corey turned around and hugged me as he leaned back to take a swig. I held my son tight and listened to him quaff down the liquor. It was the wrong time to question him about what's going on with him and my uncles.

"He's here, Mom," Corey proclaimed.

"He is here," I assured him, "Chane's always here with us in spirit, okay."

I took the bottle from my son and took a swig myself, "okay?"

Martin stood with his back against the door angrily staring me down, "For real, Mom?"

Maybe I am telling him the wrong thing. But, if it's helping him not to run from us or drink so much and feel content with his brothers' death. Then, I'm all for it. Honestly, I believe my son is always with me in spirit. I think I can feel him, too.

"It's true, son," I told Martin, "Although, I can't see his face...I know my baby is here with me."

Martin dropped his head and said nothing more to me, "Let's just all stay in here and pull out some movies."

We all took a place and made ourselves cozy. Rodney watched as Martin walked over to the television and popped in a tape. Corey spread out across my bed with his head rested in my lap while we waited for the movie to rewind completely. I comfortably leaned back on a few pillows then tossed a couple more down toward the edge of the bed with Rodney and Martin. Once we were able to press play and watch the program, Martin sparked the first of many blunts that he and Rodney had quickly rolled up. Corey and I passed the same bottle back and forth until the last drop. My boys and I sat in a trance watching the flick. Before long, I went down to the marble kitchen and made an abundance of snacks to take back up one side of the long flight of stairs. There were so many things to cook up that I made a few trips and some special orders. For hours, we watched films together and enjoyed the time. Thank God. Today started out so crazy, but at least it will end peacefully.

Martin and Rodney had fallen asleep during the last tape we popped in, so I put in another and got comfortable on my humongous bed with each of my boys. I pulled the blanket up over Corey's shoulder in an attempt to tuck him in. Though, he softly placed his hand on mine and stopped me.

"I'm still watching tv with you, Mom," Corey slurred.

"I'm sorry," I said settling into the covers, "I thought you were sleep, son."

Of course, we're still drunk and it may not be the best time to talk about anything. But, I need to know what the hell is going on. I need to know what's up with Corey and my uncles.

"Corey?"

"Hmm," he lifted his head to look at me, "Yeah, Mom."

"How did you find them?"

He sat up and propped himself up against the pillows, "They found me, at Grandma's house."

"What did they tell you, son?"

"They showed me pictures of them with Grandma Terry and Grandpa Charles," he began, "Then, they told me that Grandma Terry didn't want them to find you."

I didn't ask him anything else. The conversation faded out under the commotion from the television set. I stroked Corey's head as he dozed off and I fell into deep thought.

# Trouble in the Morning

The phone was ringing profoundly, so much so that I was woken up out of my sleep. I quickly rolled over to snatch the phone from the receiver before the ringing woke up my boys.

"Yeah," I started, scrambling for a comfortable position, "Hello."

"Stacy, baby?"

"Sam? Is that-," tears crowded my eyes as I slapped a hand over my mouth, "Is it you?"

"Don't cry baby please," he pleaded, "I know, okay I know everything…your Dad is here with me. He told me what Terry did to the house, so make sure you press charges on her ass."

"My uncles, Ricky and Lonnie, Dad's brothers brought us to my Dad's house," I informed him, "We've been here for days and we rarely see them."

"Okay, where's my boys?" Sam wondered his voice frantic, "How are my boys doing?"

"The boys are asleep, Sam, it's early."

"Wake them up," he urged, "I want to talk to them."

"Why didn't you call as soon as you could after court?" I questioned.

"I couldn't stand to hear your voice and not be right there with you, I should've did better, Stacy," Sam expressed with a deep sigh, "Your Dad knows about me and your Mom."

"What?" I exclaimed, "How does he know that?"

"I'm sure it was your mother that told him," He confessed, "If anything happens to me, Stacy, move on...I want you to be happy."

"I love you, Sam," I said breaking down once again "Nothing is going to happen to you."

"Be strong for me baby," he coaxed, "Be strong for the boys."

"Sam..."

"Don't cry, Stacy," Sam said emotionally, "where are my boys?"

"Boys, wake up!" I yelled, "Wake up your daddy is on the phone!"

Like a newborn baby Martin rolled out of the blankets, Rodney jumped out of his sleep and Corey scurried out of the bed to quickly snatch the phone from my hand. I sat there dumbfounded as the boys had a long talk with their Dad. Why would she tell him that? I mean, I'm a grown woman whatever happened is now in the past. So, I'm sure if my mother did tell my Dad he would've probably fought Sam over that by now. The boys wrapped up their conversation with Sam and hung up the phone.

"He ran out of time," Corey told me, "He said he'll be calling us again soon."

My mind kept thinking back to what my uncles said when we first got to this miserable palace. My mother kept my father from me and the money, too. I'm convinced that she wanted this house, but he left it for me, the cars as well as the rest of the money. Luckily, she never got her hands on any of my things. Now, my boys and I can live. They each fell quickly back to sleep as my thoughts kept me awake for a little while longer.

The sun shines beautifully throughout my room. I truly feel like a princess waking up in such a huge place. My boys were each comfortably scattered around my giant bed, sound asleep. I carefully climbed over Corey to get out of the bed and turn off the television set. The pixel covered grey screen screamed at me as I snatched the cassette tape out the mouth of the VCR. Happy that the boys slept through the noise, I made my way down into the kitchen. Thinking back, there was a time in my life when nothing was in the fridge, aside from an old pizza and a flat can of soda. Surely, a nice big breakfast would make us all feel a little more like we were at home. I hope that Lonnie and Ricky stop by today. So, I was sure to include them when making breakfast for the boys. One by one, they filed down the stairs and filled a seat at the table.

"Good morning, Mom," Martin said happily.

"Morning, Mom," Rodney happily expressed, following close behind Martin.

A few minutes later, Corey came down the stairs to me and first kissed my head before he sat at the table without another word. He's still pissed off about what Ricky said to him, but he wasn't saying anything wrong. My uncle made a good point. I brought the remainder of the food to the table and took my seat next to Corey. Before we got the chance to bless the food Corey dug in. Martin, Rodney and I glared across the long table at him reaching and grabbing at the food. I glared over at Martin and could see that he was ready to explode.

"What's wrong, Corey?" Martin blurted out.

Corey cut his eyes at Martin and continued to fill his plate.

"There's plenty of food, baby," I said with a sigh, "Thank you, God, for our meal. Amen."

"Amen," Rodney responded.

My plate wasn't nearly as full as Corey's, neither was Rodney's. Martin didn't touch a thing, he wouldn't let up. Martin waited for Corey to answer him and grew angrier and angrier every second that Corey didn't. For a moment, everyone was silent and the sound of forks clanking on plates filled the air, intensifying the tension.

"Bro, what's going on with you?" Martin pressed.

"We're worried about you, son," I interrupted, dropping my fork, "Are you okay?"

Corey picked up his head and allowed us to have a short glimpse into his tired eyes. He looks worse than he did when Chane died. He completely ignored us and continued to eat his food. Rodney sat in silence and continued to eat as well. I know he didn't know what to do or exactly what to say, but I need all the help I can get at this point. Corey needs to know from all of us that we love him and he's not alone.

"Son!" I slammed my hand down on the table and my eyes crowded with tears, "Please! Say something."

"It's only us…" Martin angrily expressed, "…why are you doing this?"

The one thing I don't want to do is make my baby feel like we're backing him into a corner. I know why he's angry, though I wonder myself why they accepted Rodney as their brother. The resemblance is uncanny, but he's still a stranger in the place of my child. As Chane's keeper! To keep his spirit alive!

"Don't let what Ricky said yesterday upset you," I told him, "He doesn't really know us."

"What'd he say?" Rodney finally cut in.

"Whatever he said what does that have to do with us?" Martin exclaimed.

"It should've been me," Corey murmured.

He left one last bite on his plate, dropped his fork and rested his head in his palms. Martin quickly stood to his feet.

"Call him, call him right now and I'll ask him what happened myself!"

My son moved so swiftly he practically glided across the marble floor to the phone on the wall. Corey picked up his head once again to watch Martin rant as Rodney spun around in his chair to look back at Martin in amazement. I could barely stomach watching my baby have a meltdown. Martin quickly picked up the phone from the receiver.

"Give me his number!"

"Son, calm down, please," I coaxed, "Put the phone…"

"Give it to me now!" Martin demanded.

Martin fought the tears as best as he could until he snatched the receiver from the wall and roughly slammed the phone to the hard floor. We were all shocked. Rodney and Corey sat at the table like zombies just watching him.

"You don't want to give me the number?" He asked in a threatening tone.

"Son, please, I need you to calm down," I begged, on the verge of tears.

I started to come toward my baby boy with open arms, but when I got too close he broke free from my grasp.

"No! Fix this!" Martin screamed, with his finger pointed directly in my face.

"I'm trying, son, I..."

"No!" He began to breakdown crying again, "Fix it! Fix him!"

Rodney stood to his feet and came over toward us. He stood alongside of Martin and wrapped an arm around his neck. Rodney patted Martin on his back.

"Martin, bro, what can she do? Honestly."

"I know what to do," Martin assured him.

Martin wriggled out of Rodney's embrace and made his way up one side of the elaborate staircase then down the hall. I stood in the kitchen glaring at the back of Corey's head as he sat at the table completely oblivious to the whole ordeal. Rodney followed behind Martin up the stairs and then right back down into the kitchen. Martin had the phone and receiver from my bedroom wrapped up in his hand. He stood so close to me when he screamed the heat of his breath brushed against my forehead and splatters of saliva spread across my face like misty drops of morning dew.

"Now, no one can call!" He screamed at me again, "Don't even let them in when they come knocking!"

It's like I'm the only one here and I don't know what to do. Martin fell to his knees before me, on top of the broken phone pieces. Completely letting his emotions go. My baby boy reached up and grabbed me by the hand. I sat on the floor next to Martin, happily wrapping him in my arms.

"DAD!" he screamed to the top of his lungs, rattling the drums of my ears.

All I could do was hold onto him tighter. This is my fault and no fault of mine at the same time. Corey finally got up from the table to join Martin and I on the floor. Sam is in prison, just when we finally have the money to live. This isn't living, every passing day brings more and more stress. I used my shirt to wipe away the snot from Martins' nose. Corey's strong arms wrapped around the both of us and squeezed us tight.

"I'm sorry," Corey spoke in a low undertone.

"I need you, bro," Martin cried, holding onto his brother tight.

"I'm here," Corey reassured him.

"Please, Corey, I need you to be okay, man," Martin explained, "What did Ricky say?"

I lifted my head to peer over Corey's shoulder at Rodney. He sat at the kitchen table with his head hung low in shame. There is almost nothing that I can do to keep these boys happy. There's not much that I can do at this time to keep myself happy. As long as we're together it doesn't matter. When Sam calls us back, he'll be happy to hear that we're staying strong. All except for my mother, she could've killed us!

"Rodney," I called out to him, "Son, can I hug you?"

Without looking me into my eyes Rodney came over sat down on the floor and allowed me to hold him tight.

"Are you okay?" I asked him.

"Yes, ma'am," Rodney responded, staring at the ground.

Sometimes I want to ask him what's on the floor. He's always looking down. It's the wrong time to try and lighten the heavy mood.

"Come on, boys," I stood to my feet, wiped the tears and started down into the luxurious basement.

Dark liquor beckoned for me. I slid behind the bar as they each seated themselves around the edge. I scanned the bottles for which liquor would best fit the moment. A full bottle on the top shelf caught my eye. I turned to my boys and set out shot glasses for each of us.

"We can all use a drink," I joked.

"Yeah," Corey expressed with a sigh.

"I'm sorry I broke the phone, Mom," Martin told me.

"You didn't break a bone so you're just fine, son," I smiled, filling our glasses to the rim.

"I'll put your phone back tonight."

From beneath the bar, I pulled a tray full of large, fluffy buds and began rolling blunt after blunt. Trying to do everything I knew how to make my babies feel okay. I'm afraid of what's going to happen next. I have no idea where any of this stuff really comes from.

This big beautiful house, the nice cars in the garage, the clothes and not to mention the money, it's all an inherited mystery.

"We'll wait to see if uncle Lonnie comes by today, so they can take us to get a new one," I assured them, "Until then, we'll wait for your Dad to call."

"Go plug in the phone, Martin!" Corey urged.

"Wait," I stopped Martin, "Sit down."

Silence took over the room.

"Does Grandpa know Dad?" Martin questioned.

"I guess he does, I mean, that's what he told me on the phone," I responded unsure.

"Why hasn't Dad Called us back?" Corey questioned.

"I don't know, but your Grandfather said he will take good care of him," I shared.

I don't know what my Dad truly meant. It didn't sound like he meant it in a bad way. I know Sam said my Dad knows everything. But, what can he do? I mean they're in prison with guards. It won't be anything more than a few words. I'm sure.

"I wonder how?" Rodney added, taking a drag of the blunt.

"Does Grandpa ever talk to Grandma Terry?" Corey added.

The room got a little bit smaller. When I was just a baby, my mother told me that she would take me to see him often. As I got older, for some reason, we stopped going. Maybe she didn't, it may be that she stopped taking me with her. He would send her money for me, so I was taken care of, but I wasn't. Why did he still send her money?

"I want to call Grandma Sarah so bad," I

expressed, "She would know, she would know where your Grandma Terry is, too."

"Why don't you?" Corey urged.

"I don't want your Grandma Terry to find out where we are or how to contact us."

"She won't know if you don't tell Grandma Sarah," Martin added, "I still can't believe she would do this to us."

"There's got to be another phone down here," Rodney said, searching the dark walls for a phone receiver.

"Grandma can tell us what Grandma Terry's been doing all this time," Corey explained.

"No, Mom," Rodney said coming back to the bar, "I don't see one down here on the wall or anything."

Martin handed the blunt off to me as I glared in Corey's weary eyes, "Your smart baby, we'll wait to call her when we're sober in the morning."

"Okay," Corey agreed.

"Right now, we wait to see if Lonny will come today," I told them.

"What if they don't?" Martin questioned.

"Then, we'll take one of the cars and find a store… without losing the house."

Everyone went silent for a while. We poured another round of shots, sparked another blunt to keep the tears away.

Martin broke the silence, "What did Ricky say?"

I angrily sighed, "Son, please can we just-"

"He asked me why I wasn't my brother's keeper," Corey spoke over me, "He asked me, why Rodney?"

Rodney stole a glance at Corey then looked away. He picked up his glass, swirled the liquor around and downed the shot. I watched as Martin looked over at Rodney, then back to Corey.

"This is my brother," Martin said, "Period."

"I was about to snap on him," Corey expressed, punching his palm.

"Mom, we need to get a test to see," Martin demanded.

I choked on the thick weed smoke, "A test to see what?"

"If you gave me away," Rodney stated.

What can I say? My mind is so foggy. I passed off the blunt to Corey picked up my glass and took a shot. Then, came around the bar to pull Rodney out of the high chair. He stood with me and allowed me to hug him tight.

"I'll get the test," I assured him, glaring deep into his eyes, "We can do that, but what are the odds of you coming back to me...if it's really you."

"I think it's possible," Rodney said, "I know it's really you, Mom."

I pulled him in close and squeezed him tighter. I was all out of tears. We've been crying every day since we had to move in this place. I think it's him, too. My boys knew before I did. It makes me wonder if Sam believed so, too?

### (Doorbell Rings)

My thoughts were interrupted and there was a brief pause as we fell silent; the doorbell rang again. Martin jumped to his feet and dashed toward the stairs. My heart sank into my stomach as I scrambled around the bar and up the stairs behind Martin. Corey followed as Rodney reluctantly rushed behind.

"Martin!" I screamed reaching out to grab a hold of him.

He fumbled around with the knob just before Corey snatched him up and dragged him away from the door. Rodney stood before me clueless, I gestured for him to follow the boys down the hall as I prepared to open the door.

"Don't let them in here!" Martin screamed as Corey carried him down the hall back towards the kitchen.

Once the screams grew too faint to hear clearly, I flung the door open and allowed Lonnie and Ricky inside. My uncle Lonnie cautiously stepped over the threshold as Ricky nervously came in after. Fearful, I shut the door behind them and guided them down the opposite direction into the dining room area.

"We've been trying to call you all," Ricky began.

"Is everything okay?" Lonnie questioned.

I stifled a giggle and responded, "Yes, everything is fine."

I hope Corey has got a good grip on Martin. There is no telling what he is capable of doing. Ricky plopped down on the plush sofa and nestled into the cushions. I seated myself next to him as Lonnie settled into the love seat across the room.

"We need to go into town," I started, "My boys' can't stay cooped up in this-"

Rumbling footsteps encroaching on the dining room interrupted my conversation. Martin pounced into the room with his fist balled and his teeth tightly clinched as Rodney and Corey stumbled in behind him. Lonnie's expression was unchanged, he wasn't at all shocked or startled by my baby's anger. He watched Martin lock eyes with Ricky. Unlike Lonnie, he seemed threatened by my son's demeanor.

Ricky sat up and leaned in to Martin, "What's your problem, boy?"

"What'd you say to my brother?" He demanded of Ricky.

Lonnie stood to his feet to cut in, "Hold up now, youngblood-"

"What'd you say?" Martin shouted.

"Son, calm down," I stepped in, "Lonnie, Ricky I think you should go."

"No," Ricky demanded as he rose to his feet, "Let him say what he has to say."

Corey rushed past Martin and lunged at Ricky. He wrapped his big arms around my son picked his slim body up and slammed him to the ground. It seemed as if the entire house rumbled while the glass chandelier clanked, swinging back and forth. A hush fell over the room before everyone erupted in response.

"Yo!" Martin hollered before rushing to strike Ricky.

Corey scrambled to his feet and began to attack Ricky, too. I stood by with my feet glued to the floor, shocked! I had no idea what to do. Frantic, I leaped into action and attempted to pull my boys off this big, sweaty man before he explodes. Lonnie tried his best to toss the boys aside without harming them, but they kept coming back striking blow after blow. Ricky pushed back and blocked every punch he could. The dining room table was moved out of place and my china glasses were knocked out of the shelves.

"Alright now, that's enough!" Lonnie screamed, "Get your kids!"

"Don't say nothing to my, Mom!" Corey shouted before throwing another punch at Ricky.

"NO! Just stop, son, please!"

I looked around for Rodney to help, but he wasn't here with us. Drained of all hope, I continued to pull the boys off Ricky. The next thing I knew I was flung back with such force I didn't realize I had fallen until I hit the ground. Ricky pushed back immensely. Martin landed directly on top of me. I painfully tried to get up as I attempted to hold my baby boy down. Ricky rose up and snatched Corey up by his neck lifting him up inches from the ground.

"Listen to your mama!"

"Mom!" Martin yelled, "Let me go, Mama!"

Lonnie wriggled between the two of them, "Let him go, Rick."

### (Gun Cocks)

Everyone froze as Corey stumbled to his feet coughing terribly. All at once we turned our attention to Rodney. Now, I know there's no coming back from all this. Rodney has no expression on his face, a gun in his hand and nothing more to lose. We didn't trust Lonnie or Ricky to begin with. Especially, after Martin told us that their silver truck was the same truck chasing him down. They seemed to have magically showed up just in time. First, Chane. Then,

Sam went to prison. The house got burned down and we were given this one. It's not a coincidence. I refuse to believe it is.

"Get out," Rodney finally spoke in a low, cold tone.

Lonnie turned to me with a look of disgust, "So, this is what you want?"

"GO!" Corey urged, massaging his throat.

Martin helped me to my feet as I held onto him for dear life. Ricky chuckled under his breath. Lonnie nodded his head in disbelief. They each went to make their way down the hall as Rodney and Corey followed behind. To be sure they leave and drive away completely. Martin wriggled from my grasp and rushed behind them. I glanced around at the huge mess before retreating down the hall and to the front door behind my boys. We each stood by waiting for them to cross the threshold, so we could shut them out forever.

Ricky turned to me with a devilish smirk, "Now, ya'll don't have nobody."

"If you come back I'll call the police," I threatened.

Lonnie laughed from the other side of the door and nervously rubbed down his beard. Anger consumed me as I pulled and shoved my boys away from the door. Ricky scoffed just before I slammed the door in their faces. I listened for the engine to start before turning to face my boys.

"I'm sorry, M-," Corey began.

Before he could finish, I scooped my big baby up in my arms and thanked God he wasn't seriously hurt. Forget about what he did. I'm just glad Ricky didn't kill them! Corey's slender body compared to my uncles' wide physique is more than enough reason to believe he'd break my child in half. I glanced over Corey's shoulder at Rodney peering out the window; his expression still blank.

"Rodney, look at me, son," I told him.

He left the window and rushed to my side, I let go of my big baby Corey to hold onto my other child. If he believes he's mine and I think it at times. Then, he is. I don't need a test to tell me that.

"I'm glad you didn't shoot."

I kissed Rodney on his forehead then held Martin for a while as he wiped the tears from my eyes. I took a step back and placed both hands upon my head. My teeth grinded and gritted as I tried to hold back, but my face told it all. A deep, painful cry left my lips. I doubled over and put all my weight onto my knees as I stomped my foot repeatedly. If I was alone, I probably would've drank myself to sleep, but my boys are here with me. Still, I don't know what else to do. I can only cry. Cry and pray that God sees what's happening and comes to carry us all the way through it.

"Nah, Mom! Please don't cry, momma," Corey began to sulk with me, rushing back into my arms.

I held onto him tighter, "I can't lose you. What would I do? What would I do? What the hell would I-," I wailed.

"Mom, please it's okay," Martin began to cry.

Martin dramatically slid down the wall, fell into a fetal position and covered his head with his arms. My baby hid his face in between his knees and screamed for his Dad. Rodney couldn't help, but to cry. He dropped to his knees and threw himself over Martin.

"We have each other, okay," Rodney whimpered.

Somethings got to give. I have to stop crying I

can't let my boys think that I can't do it anymore. Sam is probably dead. We don't have anything else left to lose. We must get out of this house and out of this damn state. I stopped sulking and pulled myself together. Wiping the tears from my eyes as I brushed my hair back from out of my face. I let out a sigh of relief. When I stopped crying my boys did, too. They each looked to me with anticipation. Fear in their eyes, but strength in their hearts.

"I don't know what we're going to do, I don't know where we're going to go," I spoke with no expression, "But, we got to go, and we got to go now."

"Okay," Martin responded first, sniffling he jumped to his feet.

"Let's go," Corey responded quietly.

Rodney let out a deep sigh, "I'm ready."

We each stood quiet for just a moment, still sniffling as we continued to wipe tears from our eyes. Once ideas turned to plans in my mind I rushed past the boys and through the kitchen to the garage. On the wall next to the light switch were three separate sets of keys. I snatched them up and tossed one of each to the boys.

"Get the boxes," I urged, "Nothing else."

Without a word we each hoisted up a box from the basement until one truck was completely full. Luckily, we were able to fit them all. There were at least thirty boxes. We masked the boxes with dark blankets. Since Martin was my baby, I let him drive me in the black four door truck with a tint so dark you couldn't see inside during the day. Rodney didn't want to ride in blue, so he and Corey switched keys so he could take the beige two door SUV. I felt better having Corey take the biggest truck anyways, it was cramped inside. We changed our clothes and just before the sun set we left Ken Caryl for good.

We wandered around for close to an hour before finding the 'CO-470' sign. Once we hit the highway, I felt all the pressure lift off my heart. I looked over at Martin driving beautifully. He made sure to stay close behind Rodney who was close behind Corey. At first, we got lost again while on the highway. We briefly stopped at a gas station to get directions and get back on track. My heart danced around in my chest the closer and closer we got to Denver. After a couple miles we stopped by another gas station. The boys fueled up and raced off. It got so dark we can barely see anything, though once the lights of the inner city came into view we knew we were closer. The tall buildings of downtown Denver grew larger. From so far away you could still make out the beautiful blue lit sign on the face of one of the tallest buildings.

"We're almost there, Mom!" Martin happily shouted.

I cried tears of joy, "We're almost home!"

Martin noticeably shook his head, "It's not home anymore."

He's right, downtown looked so unfamiliar. It felt like I was seeing everything for the first time. We stayed in one of the finest hotels, housed each of the trucks in the buildings underground parking garage and barricaded ourselves in the room.

# Our Worst Fears

We got in the hotel by about one or two this morning and had to be out by eleven. So, we stood up all night collaborating over out next move. We should just leave Colorado for good. Though, I've been here my whole life I don't know how to just pick up and leave. I don't have a diploma nor do my children. Sam's gone. I never had my father. My mother was part time. The only person I really need to see before we go is Grandma Sarah. Chane's grave, of course, and the house just one last time. I want to see my house. My eyes burned a bit as tears began to crowd my vision. Through the blur I could see my baby boy coming to me. I shut my eyes tight and held my lips together as I nodded my head in disbelief.

"It's okay, Mama," Martin reassured me, "We'll go wherever you want to go."

"We just have to go away from here," Corey added, "There's nothing left for us."

"Chane," I responded crying, "And, the house."

Rodney stepped out of the bathroom from washing up, "We should go now."

The boys made sure we got everything from out of the room before we each filed out. I honestly wasn't in the mood to do anything, but drink. I got into the black four door truck with Martin and prayed before we drove out of the parking lot. I prayed that God would protect and guide each of my boys. I prayed that he would take the pain and fear away from their hearts. I prayed for their happiness and for Sam to be alive. I'll be content leaving Colorado as long as I get to say goodbye. God will protect and guide us through it all.

We stopped by a payphone where I called Grandma Sarah and let her know we would be coming by. The first thing we did was drive out to Fairmount. We weaved around headstones, over a bridge and far to the back of the cemetery. We didn't need the Visitor's Center I remember exactly where my baby was put down. At least I thought I knew. We got out at the block where Chane was laid to rest. I remember the building that held earns of the people that weren't put underground. There's a large tree and we were kind of close to the street. When we got there, I couldn't find him.

"Where are you, Chane?" I started to question.

I passed by ten or more headstones some of the same names in the same area. I felt that I was close by, but not quite. I started to lose hope and after about fifteen minutes I broke down and cried.

"I'm not leaving here until I find you!" I cried aloud as I brushed flowers off the headstones of strangers.

"Mom, calm down," Corey told me, "It's okay we'll find him."

"He's right here somewhere," Martin said frantically searching with me.

"Show me where you are, son," I wept aloud, "Chane! Son, I'm not leaving… help me find you."

Corey followed close behind me when suddenly, I stopped. I wiped my tears stood in the middle of the grave lots and counted twenty headstones in from the street. My finger stopped on the other side of the tree and my body started over graves and to the exact spot where my son was laying. We got to his headstone and the leaves were cleared from his slab. I knelt over my sweet baby's grave and cried hysterically. Picking off the grass from around his stone to make it look nice as the dirt absorbed my salty tears.

"Father God!" I cried, "I want my baby back, please, God! Give me one more day!"

"He's here, Mom," Corey said painfully, "Remember? He's always here with us."

Corey knelt over Chane next to me, "She forgets that sometimes, bro."

My weeping eyes locked onto Corey. For a moment, I thought that Martin was going to get upset once again. We can't stand here arguing in front of Chane.

"I know you be here with us, Chane," Martin chimed in, "I can feel you."

My frown quickly turned to a smile as I whipped my head around to look up at Rodney and Martin looming over me. Rodney had just as many tears as I did, streaming down his face.

"You knew who I was…you knew I was your brother," Rodney said aloud.

Corey and I stood to our feet as we all came together and held onto one another for dear life. We stood together a while over Chane weeping; as a family. I took a deep breath then a couple steps back, breaking the circle. Each of my boys looked to me, confused as I began to pray.

"Father God protect and be with us on our journey to make a new life filled with love, peace and positivity. Father protect my children; all my boys and no matter what Lord keep them moving in the right direction. In the name of Jesus, I pray, Amen."

"Amen," they each said in unison.

We said our goodbyes before piling back into the trucks to leave the cemetery. I felt like I was leaving my child behind. What's worse is that the heart wrenching feeling I had was familiar. Before we arrived to my Grandma Sarah's I asked Martin to honk at Rodney, so he could honk at Corey. We each pulled over just a few blocks from her house. I got out of the car to hop in with Corey and the liquor, he's been sipping since we left Ken Caryl.

"Son, please," I pleaded, "Mama needs a drink."

Without hesitation, he reached under the driver's seat and pulled out a slender, green bottle containing one of my favorite dark liquors. I slammed my door shut, got myself comfortable and popped the bottle top off. Just before we pulled off the liquor had already started to settle in me.

"This will get you right, Mom." He assured me.

Look at my baby, trying to make me smile and it's working. Corey's happy to be leaving that torcher palace just like I am, besides we need real a fresh start. Without Chane or Sam here with us there is nothing left in Colorado only painful memories. We will never see them again. My mother is out to get us over this money and now my uncles are against us, too. Therefore, I believe a change in scenery would be nice.

"Mom, if my uncles are there don't worry," Corey said, breaking the awkward silence.

"No, we leave," I responded, "Just lead your brothers past her street, so we can check first."

Corey crept past Grandma Sarah's street. Martin and Rodney, following close behind, understood right away what we're doing. I'm sure they broke their necks to look up the block at Grandma's drive-way. The butt of her car was visible from beyond her overgrown bushes. My mother's car was nowhere in sight, thank God.

"Okay, make a right go around and park up the street," I demanded.

My heart started to pound nervously. All together I just want to leave with my boys and drive away but, I can't. Not without saying goodbye. Tears streamed down my face as we came to a halt on Grandma Sarah's street.

"Come on, Mom," Corey coaxed, "It's okay."

The door flung open for me and my baby boy Martin reached in to help me out of my seatbelt. He grabbed my hand, shut the door and guided me to the house. Corey and Rodney walked behind us, keeping their eyes open for their Grandma Terry.

"We shouldn't stay here too long, Mom," Martin expressed.

"I know, son."

The four of us cut through the grass and just before we got to the walkway, Grandma Sarah met us at the door.

"Stacy!" She exclaimed.

Grandma stood frozen in the threshold. As if she'd seen a ghost she stood silent with quivering lips. After the emotional rollercoaster the boys and I just got off we weren't ready to ride again. Seeing her looking at us that way is more than words can describe. Grandma Sarah brought tears out of us all.

"Grandma," I began.

That was all I could say before I lost control. Nearly falling to my knees, though my boys held me up. My Grandma Sarah eased down the steps of her porch and came to us with open arms.

"She's on her way here," Grandma confessed, "Hurry and go now."

We hugged and kissed her as much as possible before running up the street. Suddenly, my mother's car came looping around the corner toward us at top speed. The sound of screeching tires came from behind us. My uncles were coming down the street from the other direction.

"Run!" I shouted, "Hurry!"

Like roaches we scattered out of the middle of the street. I ran as hard as I could, still watching my mother's car race toward me. Martin parked the closest to the house, so I attempted to reach him. I grabbed for the door handle snatched the door open and started to jump in. Out of the commotion came a loud crash.

"Mom!" Martin screamed, leaping out of the drivers' seat.

My mother swerved into us lodging me in between her car and the door of our smashed-up truck. I couldn't feel anything. From the waist down to my feet I felt completely numb. I almost didn't realize what just happened to me. My Uncles, Ricky and Lonnie, swerved out of her way and crashed into another vehicle on the other side of the street. My vision started to get foggy and my hearing muffled. Though I could still hear the voices of my sons, faintly. They were screaming my name but, I can't respond. I can't speak at all. My mother backed her vehicle away as my limp, motionless body fell to the gravel. Like a coward, she sped away from the scene.

"They ran," Martin yelled out, "Help me get, Mom!"

"Grandma Sarah called the police," Rodney exclaimed, "We have to hurry and go."

My Grandmother rushed over to us. Neighbors began to crowd around asking questions and calling the police as well. With the last bit of energy, I had I tried to speak. I looked to Corey; the words stuck in my mouth.

"Son," I started, barely able to breath, "Go now!"

"No!" Martin cried, "I'm staying with you."

My eyes grew angry as I gritted my teeth. Urging my boys to take my advice.

"Now!"

"Boys," Grandma Sarah interrupted, "Go."

They each hugged her. Corey and Rodney drug

Martin to the only vehicle we filled up with money and tore down the street. They were out of sight in no time. Before the police had arrived on the scene my babies were over a half mile away. They'll take care of each other and they know that God is going to take good care of me.

# Sandbridge Beach, Virginia

After six long months of hiding in the depths, the boys were finally able to seek closure. They went from city to city and state to state trying to escape the past. Using bums and crackheads along the way. They were able to use their street knowledge to stay together and find a nice place to settle down in Virginia. Grandma Sarah died of a heart attack two months after they left Colorado. Now, they only have each other and enough money to last. Three-hundred thousand dollars in cold hard cash. Still, it wasn't enough to keep Corey up in his spirit.

Martin and Rodney sat out on the patio overlooking the sandy beach. Corey, fresh out of his afternoon nap, came out of the house stretching and yawning. A white silk robe draped over him.

"How'd you sleep, bro?" Rodney questioned.

It took Corey a moment to respond as he fiddled around in his pockets for a lighter. He lit his ritual blunt took in a deep pull of marijuana smoke and exhaled.

"Good."

"Life is good," Martin jumped in, "That's what Mom wanted for us."

Corey scrunched up his face trying to hold back the tears. He took another dramatic pull of the tightly rolled blunt then passed it on to Rodney. Corey got up from his seat and slowly made his way back inside. Scooting along wooden planks in worn down loafers.

"Corey," Martin called out to him.

Corey doubled back just before crossing the threshold. He peeked over his shoulder at Martin's tearful eyes.

"I love you, bro," Martin spoke emotionally, "It's only us."

"We have a new life," Rodney added, "We got to love it."

A tear fell from Corey's eye and without another word he rushed inside. Sliding the door shut behind him.

"We did lose a lot, Martin," Rodney said with a sigh.

Rodney dropped his head in his palms and let a few tears burst from within his soul. Martin turned his attention to the sky and silently allowed tears to stream down his face.

"They got what they deserved," Martin broke the awkward silence.

Rodney nodded his head in agreement, "Crazy right."

"What would be crazy is if Rick and Lonnie end up locked up with Grandpa Charles," Martin told him, "He got pops...he's probably going to get them, too."

"I hope so," Rodney added, picking his head up.

"We have to keep watching the news," Martin added, "They'll say-"

**Bang!**

M artin and Rodney each jumped out of fear. The sound of a single shot and tumbling following that caught their attention. They both rose to their feet and dashed inside. Beyond the island in their open kitchen lay Corey's bloody body on the floor.

"COREY!" Martin screamed at the top of his lungs.

Rodney doubled back and placed both hands on top of his head.

"COREY!"

Consumed by my own thoughts.
I'm stuck inside of my own head.
When I lay down to sleep.
I can never go straight to bed.
So, I made a pallet on the ceiling.
And, cried tears like rain from the sky.

*I asked someone to help me down.*
*But nobody was there.*
*So, I stayed stuck inside my thoughts.*
*As I remained up in the air.*

## IN LOVING MEMORY OF MY DEAREST FRIEND
## YOU WILL ALWAYS BE APART OF MY FAMILY